JOE
THE
CARPENTER

By

DAVID FALCON

Chapter 1

It was cold. Judea can get cold in winter, and today, Bethlehem was covered in a thin blanket of white.

Jacob, a carpenter, overlooked this anomaly because business was thriving with this new guy, Herod, in charge. Finally, there was someone with a vision who needed skilled labor. As cold air filled his lungs between long pulls of the plane, the curls of wood shavings echoed the perfect sharp edge of the tool. A snowflake fell into his eye, and he wiped it away with a smile. Working with your hands outdoors was the only way to earn a living. Life was good.

As the sun rose, the snow started to melt into the perfect consistency for snowballs. Jacob's son, Joseph, was playing with his friend Barbee and seized this rare opportunity to conduct target practice on several jars lined up against a wall. Barbee was a street urchin who occasionally visited but never overstayed his welcome. The boy would bring a much-needed nail or other materials found while roaming the streets to Jacob. In exchange, the little boy got some food as a reward. Afterward, he would play in the street with Joseph for a while. Informally, Barbee referred to his best friend simply as "Joe."

A young Roman soldier, just stationed in Judea, was walking down the street smiling to himself. This was his first experience with snow, and the frost got into his sandals and tickled his toes, making him giddy.

"Out of my way, Jew!" the soldier bellowed, trying to sound authoritative while pushing Barbee aside. The boy scowled as the soldier passed. Being born from slaves of Aksumite descent had given the boy a sense of pride, and he resented being called a Jew. Now that he was on his own, living on the streets, he was free, and no one could tell him what to do.

Before Barbee could stop himself, a snowball packed with a stone flew toward the Roman's helmet and hit it with a clang. As the soldier turned to face his attacker, Barbee ran away, leaving Joe all by himself.

"I'll have your head for that, Jew!" the soldier exclaimed while placing his hand on the sword that hung by his side.

"What is the trouble, Centurion?" Jacob asked, hearing the commotion from his workshop that faced the street.

"This boy needs a lesson, and my sword will teach!"

"Please, take these coins and let me deal with him," Jacob pleaded, taking his son by the hair. As the soldier held his hand for payment, he suppressed a smile. Having done similar pranks in his childhood, the incident was funny, something he would have done in his youth. Unfortunately, a crowd had gathered, and these subjects, now under Roman law, had to be taught discipline.

"So, we will add bribery to the list of offenses, Carpenter? The king has had enough disrespect from you, and examples must be made. I'll be back with my regiment at noon. Prepare your fate while you have time." As the soldier left, coins in hand, he chuckled. First, the snow, and now this. What a pleasant day; his first experience keeping the peace was fortunate. He had no intention of returning, but Joe's father did not know that. This threat was taken seriously, and Jacob had witnessed too many Jews being taken away recently, never to return.

"Joseph, why did you do such a thing?" Jacob asked.

"It wasn't me! Barbee…"

"Say no more, son. Come, we must pack and leave before the soldiers return."

As they prepared to leave, Barbee sat sobbing on a wall some distance away. He was sorry for hurting the only relations he had since the death of his parents put him out on the streets. Now, he would be alone in the world again. Deep inside, resentment grew to hatred for the Romans and anyone else in authority. The event changed his life forever.

Chapter 2

It was over thirty years since Joseph and his parents left Bethlehem. Now, a carpenter like his father, "Joe," son of Jacob, was doing well in Tiberias. He courted and married a woman called Sarah, and they had four sons and two daughters. As the family prospered, they would take vacations to the Sea of Galilee, which was not far away. During the summer, the family would spend days at a secluded cove where Joseph could enjoy his favorite pastime of fishing as the family swam naked and basked in the glorious sunshine far away from prying eyes.

Joe liked to invent and improve upon things. He braids his daughter's golden hair to make a strong fishing line nearly invisible in water. He carved hooks out of small bones and experimented with different baits. As he fished, Joe occasionally looked at his family with a smile and a wave. After a few days in the sun, Sarah always developed a tan that accentuated the curves in her body, and it was pleasant, not to mention rather sexy, to observe at a distance.

Joe tried to cast into a deep pool several yards away from the shore each year. He could see schools of fish in the depths, but the distance was out of reach. He spent hours carefully stacking rocks to form a jetty so he could walk out toward the deep pool. He kept the rocks under the surface to ensure no one else found his pier, making the rock structure invisible to the undiscerning eye. Finally, after many seasons, the jetty to his fishing hole was finished, and as he walked to the end of the pier for the first time, his daughter exclaimed.

"Look, Daddy is walking on water!" she said as the family cheered and waved. Joe waved back, smiling; these were the best days of his life.

It's only natural that children want their own lives as they age. Eventually, the siblings get married and move away. Loved ones die, gravity sets in, we get round in the middle, and receding hair turns gray. Many hard-working, middle-aged, blue-collar men remove these inevitable facts from their minds with alcohol, and Joe, sitting in a Nazareth bar one day, was no exception.

"You should have seen her," Joe told David, the local bartender, who listened inattentively while unsealing a jar of olives. David placed the olives in a bowl before his patron, hoping the snack would shut him up. "She had this tan, just like when a chicken breast is cooked to perfection—light brown fading to a creamy white."

Before Joe could complete his sentence, a man entered the establishment, and the place became quiet; all conversation stopped. The newcomer was black as coal, with a full head of curly hair slightly touched with frost. His muscular build was accented by silk robes that fit him well. A handsome face, cleanly shaven, exposed gleaming white teeth as he smiled while carefully scanning the bar before sitting down.

"Ahh Jesus, right on time as usual. Here's my monthly contribution, you dog," David said while staring down the unwelcome visitor and throwing a sack of coins onto the bar.

"I am what I eat, David. Now bring some wine for my despondent friend and me here," the new customer said jokingly while sitting down and looking over at the middle-aged man sitting alone at the bar. This patron was a stranger to Jesus Barabbas, a tax collector who made it his responsibility to know everyone in the district. "I know that voice," Joe said as he took an olive from the bowl and turned to examine the newcomer. His eyesight was not as good as it used to be, and the room's darkness didn't help, but this man sounded familiar. "Barbee? Is that you?"

"I don't believe it. After all these years, Joe?"

The two men embraced for a long time as the other patrons watched with disdain. How could anyone be happy to see a revenue agent for the Romans?

"Well, bless my gray beard, Barbee. It's so good to see you again! But why did the barkeep call you Jesus?"

"The answer is quite simple. Enslaved people were never known by their first names."

"Then you are a…."

"Was, now I am a publican here on business."

The friends sat down, and more wine was poured. David threw a few plates down with some hummus and bread onto the counter. Barbee looked at the food and thought of many years ago when he would have gone hungry if not for Joe and his family's hospitality.

"I'm sorry, Joe," Barabbas said after a moment of silence. He was thinking back to the awful thing he had done that caused his only friend to flee.

"No worries, Barbee. Dad said it was a fortunate circumstance, and we ended up all right. He always complained about the taxes in the city…"

"*Were* extensive?" David asked while cleaning a goblet and giving Barabbas a nasty look.

"Come, let us sit in a corner where we can talk privately," Barabbas said while staring down the bartender. After moving to another table, Barabbas placed his back on the wall to watch the room. As they ate, Barabbas listened intently as Joe spoke of his exile north and settling in a new town known as Tiberias, where his father prospered. Joe eventually took over the family business and became a carpenter.

"She had this tan, just like you see when a chicken breast…" Joe broke off and started to sob into his empty goblet. He missed his wife Sarah so much. With the family scattered, Joe wandered aimlessly, working only when he needed money. Without family, there just wasn't much to live for. Barabbas listened in silence, respectful of his friend's remorse. When Joe finally got a grip on himself, Barabbas spoke up.

"It is so hard to see you like this, my friend, struck down in the prime of life. Why, look at you, a handsome man with much to offer! What you need is another wife."

Joe sighed. "I was happy being married to Sarah. When she died, a part of me went with her."

"Then let's get you out there again. Life is short, and spending it in a bar reminiscing is not living. Leave everything to me." With that, Barabbas got up and left his friend with a promise to find the man a perfect second wife.

Chapter 3

Joe walked down a narrow street with Barabbas on a fabulous spring day. Shopkeepers glared as the two friends walked by and wondered who this new companion of the tax collector was. As the two friends walked side-by-side, the conversation leaned toward the matrimonial process of the time, and Joe, already married once, was not looking forward to the Jewish traditions.

"Listen, Barbee, I'm not going to stand in the temple with a bunch of other widowers looking pathetic while the priests decide who my new wife is going to be," Joe said. Like many blue-collar workers who worked in the trades, Joe was not very religious and did not attend services regularly. Temple, in his mind, was for the intellectuals with money and power. For Joe, like his father, the outdoors was his place to be with God.

"Well, let me see what I can do," Barabbas told his friend. As an escaped enslaved person, he had never attended any service or even been in a temple. The street was his church, and religion was self-preservation. "I know of a young girl who is a perfect match, and we have known each other for quite a while. Her father and I have a monetary understanding that needs rectifying."

"You mean he owes you money."

"You catch on fast, my friend, and she is cute as a little lamb just before roasting. During our last conversation, you alluded to a preference for young meat."

"Careful, Barbee, that was my wife I was talking about."

"WAS, your wife, Joe. It's time you moved on. You can't spend the rest of your life drowning in a wine jar."

"Could I see her from a distance first?" Joe asked after the conversation sank in. He was lonely, and it had been several years since he had been pleased. Barabbas was right; no one should live alone.

"Leave that to me. You will meet by chance tomorrow, here in this square." With that, Barabbas embraced his friend and walked away into the middle of the square. As he moved through the crowd, he glanced carefully from side to side, keeping his right hand on the hilt of his knife.

Joe sat under the shade of an old olive tree and thought about what he was getting into. Would this woman like him? Would he like her? When he noticed Sarah for the first time, it was love at first sight. Could he ever feel that way again? Under the tree, there was a group of small birds hopping about, pecking unseen food from the ground. The birds had each other and seemed content. It was lovely to have met someone familiar, even if Barabbas had an unwholesome reputation in town. If only Sarah were alive, but she wasn't. She was dead, and it was getting dark outside. It was time to get indoors where it was safe.

"Well, what do you think of Myriam?" Barabbas asked his friend after pointing the girl out the next day. She was getting water from a well in the square, pretending not to notice she was being evaluated.

"She is but a child!" Joseph exclaimed.

"Thirteen, to be exact, and officially a woman. Her mother confirmed the fact," Barabbas said as they watched the girl heave a bucket from the well and pour the water into a large jar.

"Excuse me for a moment," Barabbas said as he walked away just as the young girl approached. Barabbas took the girl firmly by the arm, and she did not look pleased. After exchanging a few words that did not seem to be friendly, the girl looked over to Joe blankly. Then, after much hesitation, she walked toward Joe while Barabbas went to collect taxes from a vendor by the old olive tree.

Joe suddenly got nervous upon seeing the young girl approach. Even though this kid was young enough to be his daughter, he was always shy around the opposite sex. The sun was bright, and birds sang and flew about the square. As they were just about to meet, something dropped out of the blue sky. Joe felt the top of his head, looked at the giant white mess in his hand, and started to swear.

The girl laughed, and it was pleasant to hear—a sound Joseph had not heard in a long time—an actual, genuine laugh.

As he looked into the girl's face, he smiled despite himself.

"Come, let me wash that out by the well," she said, smiling back.

Joe lay down on a stone by the well, and the girl gently washed the droppings away. As she did so, Joe felt a calmness come over him as she passed her fingers through his thinning hair. It was as if she had special healing powers of some kind, or maybe it was just the sensation of another human's touch; he had not been touched that way for years. He let out a sigh of contentment, closed his eyes, and began to doze off.

Suddenly, a slight but deliberate slap on his face made him look up. He had no idea how long he was lying there and seemed to come out of a trance.

"My name's Myriam, sleepyhead," the girl said as Joe returned to reality and looked up. She frowned back at him, more annoyed than amused.

"I'm sorry for dozing off, Myriam. Joseph is my name," he said, sitting up. After a brief pause, her expression changed. She gave him a sidelong glance and smiled with lips slightly parted, exposing straight, healthy teeth. Her white complexion complemented her beautiful green eyes and light brown hair. She was so young, but her oval face had a touch of womanhood, especially around her jawline.

"You mean Joe, don't you? Anyway, that is what Mr. Barabbas said your name was," Myriam replied with a look of disgust on her face as she nodded toward Joe's friend in the distance.

"Which name do you prefer?" he asked, looking into her eyes. She looked up and to the side, contemplating, with lips pursed, and then answered.

"I like Joe. Joseph sounds so formal."

"Joseph was the formal name given to me by my parents. Friends call me Joe, you are Myriam, correct? Thank you very much for washing the crap out of my hair."

"Such filth. Your mouth could use a good wash, too, not to mention the rest of that body!" Myriam said as she picked up the jar full of water, placed it on her head, and walked away without looking back.

Barabbas watched the encounter with approval; by the looks of things, the meeting had gone well. Myriam, however, had no intention of making this arrangement easy. She was thinking of her father and how the marriage would help out his predicament, nothing more. This Joe, chosen to be her husband, was old, filthy, unkempt, and had hair growing out of his nose and ears. Unfortunately, relationships were arranged, and she accepted the fact with a sigh. Still, while carefully moving about the busy street, the heavy water jug occasionally spilling water on her head, Joe did have a nice smile. But why was he keeping company with such an awful person as Mr. Barabbas?

Joe sat down again by the well and drank deeply, trying to sober up. A puddle left from the encounter with Myriam presented the mirror image of a disheveled old man, and he did not like the person staring back from within the reflection. Joe decided it was time for a change. He was going to get in shape, start combing his hair, and wash away the smell he had not noticed was his own until now. Something changed; his heart was beating fast. Tomorrow was finally something to look forward to.

Chapter 4

“Well, I pulled a few strings, but it looks like you are getting a new wife, old jackal,” Barabbas said as they sat under an old olive tree in the square, eating lamb kabobs from the street vendor. Joe noticed that his friend never paid for anything but was always given money whenever he approached a businessman of interest.

“What about the high priests? Even under Roman occupation, they have the last say when it comes to Jewish matrimony.”

“True, but this is a special circumstance. After all, I have a few unfriendly faces in high places that owe me certain favors.”

Joe wondered what these “favors” might be to circumvent the traditional matrimonial process, but he decided not to ask.

“Let us drink to the new wife,” Barabbas said as they walked to the local bar.

“And our fathers,” Joe added as they sat by the wall at their usual table.

“A toast to your father, who loved me like a son!”

“My father always thought you a rascal and said nothing good would ever come of you!”

"Well, father knows best! A toast to your father but not to mine," Barabbas said while thinking back to his childhood.

"Why not?" Joe asked.

"My mother was enslaved, and eventually, I came into being. I can't remember exactly by age three or four, I was to be put up for auction. Mom intervened and was cut down and left to rot in the streets. I ran away, and that was when I met you."

"You never mentioned that when we were kids," Joe said with a look of horror. Human trafficking was just a fact of life, but he never actually knew someone who had gone through the ordeal. Now, it was personal and, therefore, wrong.

Barabbas felt relieved to tell someone what had happened finally. After all these years, it felt good to drink with a friend who did not judge him for what he had become: a loyal servant of the Roman government but also the scum of Jewish society.

"Anyway, it doesn't matter now. Today, I take what I want from those who took everything from me. A born tax collector is what I am," Barabbas sighed. Secretly, he was jealous of Joe's life: loving parents, a wife, and children.

They now drank in silence. The men pondered their lives as the bartender brought olives, bread, and hummus to the table. Joe now understood why his friend behaved the way he did. Compared to Barabbas, Joe had a good life, so who was he to judge? It was a cruel world, and you did what you needed to survive.

"So why haven't I been able to see her again?" Joe asked as he walked next to Barabbas during the daily rounds of collecting taxes throughout different parts of the city. The store owners and street vendors began to accept that this new person who shadowed the Barabbas must be another publican.

"It's all good in good time, my friend. Unfortunately, the high priests are unhappy with the father's decision not to follow tradition."

"Well, maybe if I spoke with Myriam's father?" Joe asked.

"Good heavens, you must not do that."

"Why not?"

"Well, it is a little premature right now. Be patient."

Weeks passed, but Joe was not idle. With the prospect of a new wife, he took a lighter step while preparing for his second chance at matrimony. The joyful hope of having someone to talk to, confide in again, and make plans for the future made him giddy and excited. A new dwelling would need to be found, serving as a home and a business. His present digs were small and somewhat unkempt. As for wedding preparations, he decided to wait for Myriam's opinion before making any reservations or significant purchases.

Interestingly, out of all the emotions Joe felt, he never once thought about the upcoming wedding night. Somehow, when his mind wandered toward Myriam and that pretty smile, he returned to Sarah and how innocent she was. Then, thoughts would turn to her death. God had taken Sarah away, and he resented that. Would God take Myriam away as well? As Joe mentally battled with the sad memories of his loss, melancholy set in, and he found himself seated once again at the bar, drinking until he stopped remembering.

Months passed, and Joe had not seen or heard of his friend. Barabbas disappeared, and he wondered if the childhood friend had played a trick and taken Myriam for his own. Then one day, while sitting at the bar attempting to toss olive pits into a jug across the room, much to David's annoyance, Barabbas walked in.

"There you are, my friend. I have been looking far and wide for you," Barabbas said while sitting down and pouring himself a glass of wine. Joe was not convinced his friend had looked far and wide; there was a sinking suspicion that something was amiss in Barabbas's manner.

"Yes, here is your friend. What do you want, Barbee?"

"Now, now, don't be so cross. I was doing my best to take care of a circumstance that would benefit you. Unfortunately, some issues with Myriam's father and the high priests have caused delays, but don't worry. I have it all arranged now."

"What have you done, Barbee?" Joe asked. Something about his tone made him sit up and put the olive pits down, much to David's relief.

"Well, to get everyone to agree without making such a fuss about the ceremony and whatnot, I sort of mentioned that Myriam might be with child and that a discreet marriage would be more suitable."

"What!" Joe exclaimed. He could not believe what he was hearing. Then he started thinking about how Barabbas and Myriam had not been around for some time. Maybe there was more to the coincidence that was being said. "Barbee, I am not going to get involved in this. I never touched the girl, and everyone knows this. There is no way I will marry the girl now; she is your problem."

"You don't have much choice in the matter, Joe. Myriam's father owed me money, and I have been generous enough to, shall we say, make it all even so you don't have to pay the standard fifty shekels to wed his daughter. You're welcome, by the way."

"This is outrageous. I have not even seen Myriam since our first encounter, let alone had the time to bed the girl. You tell her family I will not be a part of this fallacy." He stared into his friend's eyes, trying to read the man's thoughts. It was plain Barabbas knew something about this and wasn't telling everything.

"If it were only that easy, Joe. You see, Myriam has already been sent away to relatives to make sure the pregnancy is real, or not, for that matter. So, all you can do is sit back and wait. By the time all this blows over, the wedding will be a cinch, and you will have gotten what you wanted."

"I didn't sign up for this, Barbee, and I will not take a bride-to-be, pardon the pun. Anyway, it seems too much of a coincidence that you and Myriam have been away for so long with no word from either of you. Maybe you should be the one to marry her!" Joe knocked the olives on the bar to the ground in disgust as he jealously thought of his friend and Myriam together. He was about to get up when Barabbas placed a strong hold on his friend and made him sit back down brusquely.

"Hey, what's the meaning of this? You can't make me sit here against my will. I am leaving now, goodbye."

"Sit down, my friend," Barabbas said in a commanding tone. "It would not do for you to leave right now. After all, you are a wanted man."

"What do you mean, wanted, for what?" Joe said, trying to get up again. This time, he was forcibly shoved back down in his seat by a person much stronger and more adept at fighting than he was. Joe gave in and slumped in his chair.

"You forget the time you threw a snowball at the Roman guard? Your family is still wanted for assaulting a soldier. Would be a shame if the authorities found out you have not paid for the crime committed."

Joe could not believe what was being said. As he looked into his friend's eyes, he noticed a look he had never seen before. It was a vision not of triumph or happiness, just a cold, calculated stare that meant what it said. This was blackmail, and Joe was trapped.

"You would sell out your friend?" Joe asked, more shocked than hurt. He could not believe Barabbas was capable of this, but then again, he never really knew who this man was, not until now anyway.

"No, I would not do that, Joe, but I would do my duty as a publican. Now, if you played along, there would be no reason for any mention of the offense, but…"

"I get it, Barbee. So, what am I to do now?"

"All you have to do is wait until Myriam returns from her visit to the country. Who knows, maybe this whole strange affair will blow over, and she will be found not with a child as she says."

"Who is the real father then, if not you?" Joe asked with bitterness, suspecting that he would get an evasive answer from his friend.

"Supposedly, the Almighty God, at least that is what Myriam says."

"You have got to be kidding."

"Ahh, wish I was, my friend. According to Myriam, right after you two met, she had this vision regarding some Spirit that came to her in the night and gave the poor girl some story of being with child, but no ordinary child, the son of God Himself."

"She is crazy!"

"Just what we all thought. Of course, her folks blame you for the whole fiasco, and the high priests want you crucified for the offense. I must admit I had my doubts about the whole ordeal, but she insists you never touched her."

"But I didn't, except for the brief time at the well, and not even I work that fast!" Joe said, half-mocking yet pleading to get his friend to believe him.

"I know you didn't do anything, my friend, because I have always kept an eye on you whenever I was away."

"You mean you spied on me?" Joe said, trying to get up again.

"Not exactly. Now, sit down and stop interrupting. I was making sure nothing happened to you because of our relationship. The locals do not approve of my profession, so I ensured you were always protected if someone wanted to take revenge on you because of me." Barabbas stared long and hard again at his friend, but this time, it was not a cold stare but one of pity. "Joe, you have no idea how wonderful these days have been, seeing a familiar face again. The past few months have been the happiest since we played in the streets together so long ago. Whether you believe me or not, I tried to get you out of this predicament, but you were not only engaged to the girl but the only man she has been seen with."

"But this pregnancy can't be true, can it? It has to be some fantasy the girl is going through. After all, she is practically a child."

"A woman, according to the mother, remember?" Barabbas interrupted.

"Okay, a woman, but surely this is some deranged kid who—" Joe stopped midsentence as he remembered what Myriam thought about his appearance the first time they met. "Maybe she is trying to get out of the marriage?"

"Thought of that. I remembered the slap she gave you at the first meeting."

"You saw that?"

"I see and hear everything, Joe, and believe me, I wondered if she had found someone else to take your place, but she insists there is no one else and that God has given her an immaculate conception."

"That has got to prove she is insane. Can't we have the kid put away?" Joe pleaded.

"Well, she states you are not the father. So, there is either someone she is trying to protect or she is crazy," Barabbas said.

"You don't think somebody—" Here Joe stopped short and thought back to the night Sarah came home beaten up and brutally raped. She died giving birth, and the bastard stillborn died shortly afterward. Joe never recovered, took to drinking, and eventually lost touch with the rest of his family. Now, he was looking forward to starting over, and this happened. Joe kept the cause of Sarah's death to himself, like any respectful husband.

"Anything is possible, Joe. Sit tight, and we will know the truth in a few weeks."

Joe took a drink and thought about Sarah and how pretty she was. There was such life in her, always positive, generous, and giving. He never found out who had raped her. He closed his eyes, but instead of seeing his past wife, he saw Myriam's green eyes looking at him. After a while, he spoke up.

"I'll marry the girl regardless," Joe said definitively. He could not believe his words.

"You have no choice, but I am glad you came to your senses," Barabbas replied as he drained his cup and walked out.

Chapter 5

†

"It's true," Jesus Barabbas said to his friend several months later as they sat in the shade of the old olive tree. Myriam was pregnant with a child; Barabbas had seen her in person to witness the fact. Joe was going to marry a pregnant woman. Joe knew that society did not accept the situation with forgiveness or mercy.

"When will the ceremony take place?" Joe asked, but the words were like ashes in his mouth. Now that reality had set in, he was not looking forward to the arrangement, especially when he remembered that Myriam disliked his appearance. Then he held the vision of those green eyes and an innocent smile in his memory. No, something was not right here, he thought. Joe had a way of reading people, and he met enough women to know who was promiscuous and who was not. He held his hand to his cheek, remembering the slap duly given at their first encounter. Myriam had grit and did not seem like the type who would lay down against her will without a fight. Still, here he was. Myriam would have the baby, and her story had not changed.

"We have it arranged for next week. I wanted to give you time to see her and make sure you both are in complete agreement. After all, she cannot hide the fact anymore."

"Well, so much for a wedding night!" Joe said, trying to sound unconcerned. His stomach felt like a herd of camels attempting to search for a way out. "What did the parents say about the wedding?"

"They don't care; they haven't seen Myriam since she insists God is the father. Fact is, no one will be present except the Kohen and myself if you want me there."

"You would do that for me, us?" Joe said, holding back his emotions. The reality was starting to set in. He was to marry a pregnant woman who undoubtedly was insane. Joe had seen enough mentally ill homeless people wandering the streets, talking and arguing with themselves. Would this be a similar situation with his wife-to-be?

"Of course, Joe. I feel responsible somehow. You know I did not mean for this to happen this way." As their eyes met, Joe searched for anything resembling deceit. What he found was genuine sympathy. Maybe Barabbas was telling the truth. Maybe he didn't know who the actual father was.

Joe saw Myriam for the second time in a secluded courtyard. She was seated on the edge of a small pool, singing while tapping her bare feet in the water. As she splashed, Myriam sensed someone was behind her and quickly turned around.

"Well, you haven't lost your way in making an entrance, sneaking up on people, and scaring me half to death." As he came closer, however, she smiled and squinted as she looked up; the sunlight behind his back had blinded her momentarily while she sought his face.

Joe was taken aback—actually, he was speechless. This was the last way he expected them to meet. She seemed glowing, happy, and content—the same way he vividly remembered Sarah when pregnant with their first child.

"I'm sorry to have startled you, Myriam," Joe said. He was embarrassed and felt like he had done something wrong. The expression was obvious.

"I'll forgive you this time, Joe. Just sit down and let me look at you. Certainly, this is an improvement from the last time we met."

"Thanks." That was all he could say. This girl, now a woman, was pregnant but showed no signs of being crazy. She seemed more beautiful since their last meeting as if she had grown up in a matter of months.

"Just as talkative, too. It's nice to see you again, Joe. I was wondering how you would look cleaned up, and you lost some weight, too, yes?"

"You gained some," he replied with a gulp. If ever Joe had put his foot into his mouth, this was it. Half expecting to be slapped again, but harder this time, the response was unexpected. She laughed until she was red in the face.

"So, you have a sense of humor, too?" she said after taking a few deep breaths until the color dissipated from her face. There was no look of remorse, fear, shame, or anguish, just contentment.

"You look good, Myriam, healthy," was all he could say without staring.

"Thank you for the compliment," she replied, taking her feet out of the pool and drying herself before putting on her sandals.

"Pregnancy suits you." He could hardly believe what he was saying, but it was out, and he thought it was better to bring this matter up now before he lost his nerve. "How did it happen?"

"God gave me this gift of life. I am so happy, and I hope you are happy for me too. So many people don't believe me, but I knew you would understand. You do believe me, don't you, Joe?"

He watched her as she spoke the words. They were so genuine and pleasant. This was not the voice of a woman who was abused or taken advantage of. She looked like a radiant expecting mother, so full of life.

"I see someone happy to be pregnant. I have seen that look before, and yours is genuine, Myriam." That was the best he could say under the circumstances.

"So, what do you want to do now? No one is here. I made sure of it," she asked, glancing at the exit. This was it, a chance to get out of the situation. She provided an escape; all he had to do was take it and leave. But now, seeing her again, he made up his mind.

"The marriage will be next week if that is all right with you."

"That's fine with me. I am looking forward to spending my life with you, Joe. Initially, I was unsure, but now I see you in a new light, and I appreciate that you bothered to clean up."

He could not believe what she was saying. He made the ultimate sacrifice here, and she was joking about the situation. Maybe the kid was crazy, but the look on her face was comical as she waited for a response. Then, sensing the joke in her words, he laughed, which was contagious. She joined in as Barabbas, hidden behind the wall near the exit, sighed in relief, moved his left hand away from the knife sheathed in his belt, and stalked away, leaving the two alone.

Chapter 6

The following week, Joseph, son of Jacob, and Myriam were married discreetly. No one was present except Barabbas and the priest. Myriam did not seem to care, and Joe, already married once before, was pleased to have it over quickly and quietly.

After the ceremony, Barabbas escorted them back to Joe's abode. Myriam went inside, happy to be as far away from Barabbas as possible. No plans had been made for a honeymoon, and neither Myriam nor Joe seemed to care. To prevent the newlyweds from any local gossip, Barabbas came up with a plan to get them out of Nazareth to start a new life without being judged by the locals.

"I'm sorry, my friend, but that is the law. All Jews are to return to their place of birth and be counted for the census according to the king," Barabbas said as they stood outside Joe's apartment.

"But why do we have to travel so far while she is pregnant?"

"You were raised in Bethlehem, and that is the law. Myriam is your wife, and she will be counted as well," Barabbas said. The story of Myriam and Joe was causing quite a stir in Nazareth. Joe even stopped going to the local bar to prevent being questioned by David, the proprietor. Barabbas thought it wise to get them as far away from Nazareth as possible, and the census was a perfect excuse to leave town.

To Joe, he did not care about the king's order. He was being inconvenienced by this demand to be counted like so many sheep and did not want to travel so far away as Bethlehem.

"Look at it this way. If you get there before the child is born, only two and not three people will be taxed."

"You sure about that, Barbee?"

"Trust me, my friend, why would I lie to you?"

"At least I did not start a business in town and, therefore, do not need to settle up locally?" Joe expected his friend to request a payment of taxes now that he was leaving town. In the past several months, Joe has never seen Jesus Barabbas give mercy to anyone who owes taxes, and he has not asked Joe for any payment.

"Consider it a wedding gift from a generous friend. Now come with me to the back of the building. I want to show you something."

"Thank you, Barbee," was all Joe could say in reply; he did not know whether to be happy about the intangible gift or insulted. While they walked, a baying sound came from the back of the building. A Nubian donkey, well-fed and in the prime of life, was tethered to a hitching post.

"Congratulations, Joe, and best of luck to you!" Barabbas exclaimed while taking the reins and giving them to his friend.

"Oh, Barbee, what a wedding gift. This is so generous. Wait till I show Myriam. Please come in so we can thank you together. She will be so relieved to ride instead of walking on our journey."

"Thanks, but no. Better to leave with happy memories than be given the scorn of the woman who hates and despises me for what I am."

"A tax collector?" Joe asked.

"If that's what you want to call it, sure." Then, turning around without looking back, Barabbas walked away, and the friends did not see each other again for many years.

"We better leave soon, or we will miss the deadline, Myriam!" Joe said to his wife as they packed up their possessions for the long journey to Bethlehem. The winter marked the last days for people to be counted for the census, and there were only a few weeks left before Myriam was expecting.

"Are you sure we have to travel now?" Myriam was well along in the pregnancy and was expected to give birth soon. The thought of traveling on the back of a donkey for several days while pregnant was not what she was looking forward to. She was scared that she might lose the baby if the donkey threw her.

"The sooner we get on the road, the better!" Joe said while gathering up his tools in the apartment. In the past few days, he had invented a saddle that would hold his wife comfortably while offering enough space to carry their remaining possessions. Since they were married in disgrace, there was no wedding dowry, and what money Joe had was now running short. The sooner they started a new life in Bethlehem, the better. "Now, I made this rope ladder with three steps. I will hold the donkey as you climb up backward. If you begin to fall, I will catch you, promise."

"Promise?" Myriam asked while placing her heel on the first step of the ladder and pausing, reluctant to climb up.

"I promise, my dear wife. Up you go!" Myriam was a little scared and gripped her fingernails into his shoulder before she started to climb. Joe winced in pain as her long nails bit into his flesh for support. When she finally got seated, Myriam felt frightened by the enormous distance to the ground below.

"He called me wife," she whispered to the unborn baby as she gripped the reins.

"What?" Joe asked as he rolled up the ladder and arranged his tools in the back of the saddle.

"Nothing, Joe," she replied with a nervous smile as she attempted to look backward.

"You will be fine!" Joe said, attempting to read her thoughts. "I made the saddle in such a way that you can rest your back as we move along, and if, mind you, the donkey kicks or tries any funny business, I will be there to hold this stupid ass steady."

"Joe, really, still with the filthy mouth?" Myriam said while taking deep breaths and holding on for dear life.

Joe was pleased. She would have been too scared to ride in the saddle if she had not made that comment. How much he had learned about his new wife in such a short time.

It was a fine day as Myriam and Joe embarked on their journey to Bethlehem. Joe said the plan was to head south via the Jordan River. Joe used the excuse that by keeping off the main road, they would be less likely to be robbed by highwaymen. They dressed in old clothes to give the impression of being poor. Joe cunningly concealed his precious tools and their money under the saddle backrest he had made for Myriam.

The days were long and arduous, for the ancient trail wound alongside the river in twists and turns. Fortunately, they met very few people except the occasional farmer or shepherd. As they journeyed south, the baby started to kick, and Myriam became anxious and fearful of giving birth alone in the wild. During the day, Joe did his best to evade asking the questions that had started to take root and grow in his mind, specifically, who was the real father, and why wasn't she married to that man instead?

The more he thought about it, the more frustrated and jealous he became. Instead of confronting her, Joe kept the thoughts to himself. To break the silence on the journey, Joe spoke about happy times in the summer, fishing by the sea with his former family. As for Myriam, a young, inexperienced, pregnant child, she silently listened to Joe while holding on for dear life. She had not gotten used to riding the donkey and would grip the reigns in terror every time the animal would kick from excitement.

"I have to pee," Myriam said late one afternoon as the sun and temperature were starting to go down.

"Again? We just stopped a few minutes ago."

As they traveled along the trail, Joe would stop abruptly now and then to listen for bandits. Myriam was always caught off guard and plunged toward the donkey's neck. This constant jolting of her body increased her need to urinate. Once stopped, Joe would wait and keep silent, listening to make sure no one was following them. Regardless of what Myriam might think, thieves did not care if she was pregnant. They would kill Joe and take everything else, including her and the prized donkey.

"Regardless, I have to go," Myriam demanded. After so many unplanned stops along the way, Joe knew what that tone meant.

"At this rate, it will be summer before we get there," Joe exclaimed, holding the donkey. She slowly descended the ladder and gripped his shoulder tight until he winced.

"Well, you try bouncing along on the back of that animal and being jolted by your sudden, unannounced stops for no reason. We could have taken the road and probably been there by now, but you insisted on journeying in the wilderness."

"Backcountry is safer, and we always have water to drink and bathe in," Joe replied. They were about halfway to Bethlehem, and the sun was sinking fast, for days were shorter in Judea during the winter. "We might as well camp here for the night," Joe said, looking around, "as safe a place as any."

He quickly held up his hand, a signal to be quiet, and listened intently for any sounds up ahead and behind. There was a cutaway in the river and a small patch of sand. Joe looked at it for a long time; no one had been there for many days.

"Thank you for stopping, Joe," Myriam said as she returned from relieving herself and sat by a rock close to the water's edge to bathe her feet. There, they ate a meal of bread and dried goat meat. As they sat silently, Joe saw a fish break the water and yearned for his fishing pole. He lit a small fire, and they warmed themselves as the light slowly faded and darkness came upon them. In the evening twilight, a star never seen before appeared.

"Is it me, or is that a new star in the sky above us?"

"I can't say; it might be. I am so tired, and the pains from the kicking hurt. Are you sure this is normal for a child?"

"Sure, don't worry about it. Remember, I had four kids before yours. It is natural. Hang in there and try to rest." As Joe put Myriam to sleep that night, he looked at that glowing star in the distance one more time. It seemed to be getting bigger, he thought. Then, after feeding and watering the donkey, he walked around for a while, listening to the sounds of the night. Confident no one else was camping nearby, he laid down on the sandbank and slept with his back to Myriam to keep each other warm.

"It hurts, Joe," Myriam exclaimed as they were on the last day of the journey into Bethlehem. They were back on the main road, and their progress was good, but they could only go as fast as Joe could walk. He was not as young as he once was, so the pace was slow, and the sun was sinking fast.

"I hear you, Myriam. Look ahead in the distance. We can see the city lights from here. Soon, we will be lodged for the night and get you some assistance with the childbirth."

Joe was anxious. He could tell that Myriam was about to go into labor. They needed to travel a few more miles into town before it happened. The thought of her giving birth along the road was eating up his mind. Why couldn't this child of God keep it together and wait until His mom was safe and sound in a proper room? Then Myriam started to scream in pain.

"Hold on, Myriam, we are almost there, and I see what looks to be an inn up ahead." He waited for a reply, but she gave none. During the journey, Myriam quickly retorted when Joe was trying to placate her. Now, she was silent, and he knew the time had come. Quickly, he pulled the donkey, who stubbornly refused to break into a trot.

"Here is a place, Myriam. Hold on while I get a room." After much loud knocking in desperation, the door finally opened, and an innkeeper peered out. With one look at Myriam, pregnant and crying out about to give birth, the proprietor slammed and locked the door. After repeated pounding on the door, Joe gave up and moved on.

They went down a lane in a panic, desperate to find someplace that would take them in. He pleaded at each establishment while Myriam's cries grew louder.

Then, Joe's plea for help was answered at the last lodging on the street.

"Yes, what is it?" a man asked through a small hole in the door. As the owner peered out through the peephole, he could see Joe's frantic look and slid the bolt for safety.

"Please, for the love of God, open the door. My wife is about to give birth, and she needs a place to lay down."

With those desperate words, the man behind the door noticed an opportunity. When there's panic, there's profit, he thought.

"Well, you can take the girl into the stable behind the inn and stay there for the night. It will only cost you three shekels."

"What?" Joe could not believe what this man was saying.

"Please, Joe, there is water coming out of me. I am scared. Let me down."

"Is that your donkey?" the innkeeper asked.

"Yes, it is," Joe said between panting for breath.

"Extra shekel for the donkey!" the innkeeper said as he put a small wooden spoon out of the peephole to collect payment.

Joe quickly reached under the saddle, pleading for Myriam not to dismount just yet, and found his money bag. He quickly counted out four coins and placed them on the spoon. The innkeeper dropped them, trying to bring the spoon inside, so Joe had to search in the dark, feeling his hands in the dirt until he found them. With each passing second, Myriam's screams could be heard from behind, desperate and pleading.

"Thank you," replied the innkeeper from inside. "Meet you around back. It will be an extra shekel if you want light, water, and towels." Joe pulled the donkey, but it was in no mood to get along after the last few miles of exertion. Finally, after much pulling on the reins, the animal yielded and followed to the back of the inn into a filthy stable. There were several oxen inside lying in their filth while chewing their cud. Joe tied the donkey to the manger and quickly pulled Myriam down without using the ladder. By now, she was crying in pain, and she just lay down on a patch of straw. The innkeeper arrived a few minutes later with a pitcher, some dirty towels, and a lantern.

"Two shekels, one for payment and one for deposit until tomorrow when I get these items back."

Without a word, Joe gave the man the money and waited for someone from the inn to come and assist Myriam with the birth. After several minutes, Joe realized that no one was coming to help.

Around midnight, in the cold, damp stable behind the inn, Myriam gave birth to a baby boy. When Joe heard the newborn cry out for the first time, he looked up at the sky and cursed God for putting them through such torment. Then, directly above, the star that appeared days before flashed before his eyes, turning the darkness into light.

Chapter 7

"Joe, come here!" Myriam cried out now that the birth was over. "What am I to do with, with this?"

Joe approached the stable's entrance, and Myriam was visible as daylight. The light from the star above was so bright it cast shadows inside the stable.

Myriam was looking up, exhausted and confused, oblivious to his expression. In one hand was the umbilical cord, and the newborn baby in the other. Joe came to his senses, produced a knife, cut the cord close to the child's stomach, and stepped back.

He was horrified by what he saw. In Myriam's arms was a newborn baby, but one that he was expecting.

"It's—I can't believe it. It's—" Joe was stunned and could not believe his eyes. This was impossible.

"Joe, what should I do?" Myriam asked, looking down at the cord in her hand that was partially inside the womb.

"In a moment, after you have rested, pull gently, and the rest will come out of you," he said, referring to the placenta. "The stub will fall off on the baby in a few days." Again, he looked at the baby with bewilderment as Myriam held the little one in her arms. The light from the star was so bright that there was no mistaking what he was looking at.

"Joe, what's wrong?" Myriam asked as she looked at his face in the reflection of the shining star.

"Look at the boy," Joe said.

Myriam was astonished but not alarmed or surprised. Instead, she smiled, pulled on the placenta, and, in relief, sighed while asking for a towel. Mechanically, he found the cleanest rag provided by the inn-keeper, soaked it in water, and gave it to her.

"He's so small and precious," she said while wiping the child clean of humanity.

As Myriam finished cleaning the baby, there was no mistake in what Joe was seeing. The newborn child in Myriam's arms was Black.

He began to think of his friend and how he had arranged this whole affair to get them out of town before the child could be born. Suddenly, he laughed, assuming Myriam had known who the father was. Then he approached and wiped the baby's skin to see if the color would come off. Then, thinking of his friend's skin color, he said, with a touch of irony and a smile, "I think we should call him Jesus."

"Jesus, that's a fine name," Myriam said. Then she closed her eyes, exhausted from the birth, while Jesus began to cry in her arms.

Joe took the child, wrapped the boy in swaddling clothes, and placed him in the manger. Between mouthfuls of hay, the donkey conveniently breathed his hot breath onto the baby, keeping the child warm. The frost from the cold air was visible in the exhale. Then, the donkey made a distinctive sound, and an awful smell permeated the air.

"Well, that's just perfect!" Joe said while looking up and cursing at the sky. He walked out into the open to get some air. How could this be, he thought, a Black baby? He only knew of one other person who was just as Black. He was lied to; that was obvious. But why didn't Myriam confess who the real father was and stop this fallacy? Joe sat down and started to sob quietly to himself. What had he gotten himself into? No matter what, from this day forward, no one would believe that kid was his son. Up above, in the clear night, the shooting star passed by and slowly diminished out of sight.

Chapter 8

News spread far and wide about the sighting in the sky over Judea. Many eyewitnesses saw the event as a bad omen and were frightened. Panic ensued, and Rome was blamed for bringing this pestilence upon the people. The king called together all the chief priests and officials to have them find out more information. The officials sent agents throughout the kingdom to investigate this strange sighting that had frightened the people.

After several weeks of searching, the king's agents began returning with news about the star that turned night into day. During their travels, they learned that others were also seeking the location of the sighting. These individuals were from distant lands and mentioned something about a prophecy. The first part of the prophecy had come true: a star was sighted that turned night into day. The second part of the prophecy told of a child to be born under a bright star who would one day be king and bring salvation to everyone.

Once Herod was delivered this information, he grew paranoid. How could this happen? He, King Herod of Judea, was their appointed ruler. Since taking office, he had instituted many new civil projects for the public, and there was prosperity. This prophecy of a newborn king, one that would take his place, must be stopped.

Herod summoned his agents. "Bring anyone searching for the child to me so I may question them about this prophecy." The agents set out and eventually found three individuals seeking information about the star. The agents politely asked these scholars to visit the king, who wanted to assist with their quest. The scholars, not knowing the king's true intentions, agreed.

When the scholars were presented before Herod, he learned that the prophecy about a newborn king was true. To heighten the king's fear, he immediately noticed that these were wise men of learning, not just superstitious citizens. Herod asked many questions, particularly where they thought this child might be. The scholars looked at each other with questioning glances before answering. They immediately noticed the change from being questioned to being interrogated and vaguely answered that the child would most likely have been born within sight of the bright star. When the king received this answer, he said, "Please, when you have found the child, bring me word so that I may go and pay him homage."

When the scholars heard the king speak, they knew by his tone and facial expressions that he was seeking out the newborn for nefarious purposes. Once the wise men bid the king farewell, they set out quickly to reach the newborn before any Roman agents did. The wise men hired runners who set forth throughout the land to find the newborn and warn the parents to flee Judea immediately.

Chapter 9

After the birth of Jesus and some much-needed rest, Myriam and Joe entered the city of Bethlehem. The census was taken, and the newborn was counted as a third family member, much to Joe's annoyance. After paying the taxes, Joe found a place for the family to stay on the outskirts of town as temporary housing.

Myriam insisted that Jesus must be circumcised and presented to the temple per Jewish law. Joe knew there was no arguing this fact and dreaded the thought of being ridiculed by the priests. When he questioned Myriam about how they were to explain the boy's father, she replied, "God will provide the answer."

As they settled into their new dwelling, not all the neighbors were friendly. Myriam was so proud of her son and persisted in telling everyone that God was the father. As gossip spread about this strange marital affair regarding an old man, a young girl, and a Black baby, people started to loiter about to get a glimpse of the baby in its mother's arms, suckling on her teat. At first, Joe was optimistic and thought all this traffic would be good for business, but that was not the case. No one came asking for business, and eventually, he sent away anyone who approached to gawk at the mother and her newborn Black baby.

"Something has to change soon, or we will starve," Joe said one day when he returned from prospecting for work. Joe was an excellent carpenter, and his pride got the best of him. He took the dismissal personally even though he knew the real reason why he was being passed up for contract work at nearby job sites.

"Have faith, Joe, everything will work out, you'll see." To Joe, his wife was oblivious to their predicament, yet he could not shake her positive attitude. Watching Myriam with Jesus that evening, he noticed a faint glow surrounding the baby and mother, as if the bright star had left an eternal light on them both. With his eyesight failing, he shook off the halo surrounding their heads as a sign of old age. What else could explain this faint glow, he thought.

Joe eventually found work in distant parts of town far from where he lived. He stayed on the job well into the evening hours to distract himself from his predicament. Eventually, customers noticed his quick turnaround, and Joe started to get steady work to provide for the family.

"Forty days are drawing near, Joe," Myriam said one day as her husband fabricated a leather hinge for a customer who wanted a door installed at a local warehouse.

"Yes, I know, but why must we go through the ritual? After all, if Jesus is the son of God, he should be exempt and thus save us the five shekels we will owe the temple!"

"We are going tomorrow," Myriam said firmly, then sat to breast-feed the growing baby. Joe wasn't concerned about the money; it was what everyone would say about the child's color in the temple.

Then there was Myriam. No matter how he tried to convince her to remain silent about the baby's father, she would not relent. When their arguments escalated, Jesus seemed to cry to calm the parents down at just the right moment.

The day of presenting the newborn to the temple was fast approaching, and Myriam asked Joe when he would be purchasing the doves needed for sacrifice as part of the ritual. "Okay, okay, I'm going out to try these new traps I invented to catch some doves," Joe said the day before they were expected in the temple. As he walked away, he listened to the baby's cry and sighed. It felt good to get away and do something constructive that was value-added. With great pleasure, he caught several birds with his new invention and cooked a few that evening for dinner. Two live doves remained in the traps until the ceremony the next day. Even if Joe could afford it, he was not going to purchase a ram for the sacrifice of what people would perceive as a bastard child once they set eyes on the boy and its mother.

The night before the offering, Joe could not sleep. He was nervous about visiting the temple and presenting this Black baby. Customers occasionally mocked him, and many neighbors thought Myriam was crazy when she explained who the real father was. To make things worse, Myriam could not stop Jesus from crying. Joe threw a blanket over his head and tried to block out the noise while counting down the hours until daybreak, dreading every approaching second.

Chapter 10

In the temple, it did not go well. As Myriam presented Jesus, she kept to her story and insisted God was the father and not Joe. During the presentation, the priests could only laugh and agree with Myriam while looking at Joe and his pale features. "Of course, it is obvious this child is the son of God and not from the old man before us!" As the ritual commenced, a crowd gathered to witness this son of God and the eclectic parents. Several mocked the family, but a few praised the newborn earnestly.

"Let's go," Joe said as the ceremony ended. All that was left was the sacrifice of the doves. As the cages were being opened, a priest made the mistake of not paying attention, and the doves escaped and circled high above the temple. This caused even more jokes from the crowd. "Look, God is so pleased with the child that he will forgo the sacrifice!" Everyone thought this was very funny, but Joe turned red with embarrassment. Joe had explained in detail how to open his traps, but the priest didn't listen, hence the birds' escape.

As Joe and Myriam were about to leave, a man stepped forward and said, "Wait, may I hold the son of God for a moment?" Then Myriam, without flinching, handed the baby Jesus over to the man who said his name was Simeon. He held the baby up and spoke to the crowd,

"This child was conceived to be our savior; thanks be to God." Then Simeon kissed the baby and returned Jesus to Myriam. Joe was bewildered at the remark, not sure if the man was mocking them or praising the baby. Quickly, Joe headed toward the temple's exit, but not before an old woman approached and blocked their way.

"This is the child who will lead us to salvation," the old woman said, and she thanked Myriam and Joe for coming to the temple so that she could behold the son of God before she died.

"Let's get the heck out of here!" Joe said, pulling Myriam along before anyone else could say anything.

"Seriously, you swear in a holy place?" Myriam said as they walked back home.

"Those people were crazy, just like—" He quickly stopped talking and picked up the pace for home and a drink.

"Me, Joe? You still do not believe what I have told you all along? How can you doubt what others see as well?"

"Myriam, I see a loving mother in your actions, but you do not see my point of view. It will take more than a few insane individuals to convince me otherwise."

"They are coming, Joe," she answered.

"I'll bet," he replied as they walked home with Jesus crying in his mother's arms. Joe just stared forward and tried to imagine who "they" were and what would happen if she was indeed telling the truth. All Joe wanted was a normal married life, like he had long ago. It was now getting late, and when they arrived home, many neighbors gave them strange looks and quickly went indoors. Turning a corner to their home, they were greeted by three strangers waiting outside their dwelling.

"Good evening. Can I assist you with something? Repairs to a bridle, perhaps?" Joe said to the men standing beside their dwelling. To Joe, this looked promising. He had never seen individuals so lavishly dressed since Barbee. The men reminded him sharply of his old friend. Then panic set in. Those strange looks on the way home—could these men be here to arrest him, as Barbee threatened?

In a glance, Joe sized the men up. They did not look like Roman agents. No, they looked foreign, not from these parts. There was something exotic in their attire and manner. The dromedary camels in a field nearby were groomed and lavishly bridled, the guards tending the animals heavily armed. Then, to Joe's surprise, they went directly over to Myriam and bowed.

One of the wise men asked, "Is this the child born during the night of the bright star?"

"Yes, this is Jesus, my son," replied Myriam matter-of-factly. There was no surprise in her voice in meeting such wealthy men in front of her home. Then, all three men bowed down and worshipped the child. Joe blinked. Was this some bad dream? After dealing with the terrible, embarrassing incident in the temple, he just wanted to go inside, have a drink, and pass out, but now this? Like any blue-collar man faced with adversity, he desperately needed that drink now!

"We have come to pay our respects to the newborn and have brought offerings for the child!" With a clap of hands from the wise men, the guards brought gifts from each camel and presented them in turns to the baby Jesus.

Throughout Joe's entire life, he had never seen such treasures. There was gold in the form of jewelry and precious coins inside a magnificently carved wooden chest. Then, another box was presented, made from a mysterious black wood inlaid with ivory. When opened, the smell of frankincense filled the air. The third gift was presented on a deep red pillow of fabric, which was so fine that Joe wondered how it was made. On the pillow was a golden bottle containing myrrh oil. Joe could work for a lifetime and never afford a fraction of these gifts. Stunned, he watched as the presents were placed before Myriam and the child, and then each man bowed and stepped back to pay homage.

In the distance, the neighbors stood in wonder. Some were now doubting their disbelief. Maybe this child was the son of God?

After several minutes of quietly praying in their perspective languages, the wise men are interrupted by Joe.

"Can I offer you something?" Joe did his best to be a kind host to the visitors, but there was hardly anything in the home to offer except some wine mixed with water, a few uncooked doves, and unleavened bread.

"No, thank you. This visit was enough to satisfy ourselves that the prophecy was real. The son of God has come to earth."

"So, you believe this kid to be the son of God?" Joe asked, still bewildered by these visitors in their lavish clothes. He could not take his eyes off the gifts presented and wondered if they were theirs to keep. Joe decided it was best not to ask.

"You do not believe?" one of the wise men asked.

"Well, by skin comparison, he is not my son," Joe said as Myriam held Jesus in her arms and gently rocked the boy to sleep. She did not notice or even care about the gifts glittering in the sunset. Myriam knew instinctively why these men were here. They came to see the son of God, and she was pleased to present the boy to anyone, rich or poor. Then, one of the wise men stepped forward. His name was Balthasar, and he was from Ethiopia, Africa.

"Ahh, so you do not believe that God's son would be Black? Do not be embarrassed. I see the disbelief in your eyes and hear it in your words. The first man and woman created by God on this earth were Black. Through migrations over the centuries to colder climates, the skin color gradually grew lighter. We scholars have studied many different races worldwide and can attest to this. I, for one, am not surprised that the child is the color of the first race on earth," Balthasar said in response to Joe's candid words.

"Well, also there is, I mean, and uhm, we have never actually…" Joe stopped his sentence, a little embarrassed at what he was admitting. Suddenly, the wise men talked in unison, excited and joyful to hear what Joe confessed. He stood there dumbfounded and a little embarrassed, for several languages he did not understand were being spoken. When the conversation ended, another man, Melchior, from Persia, talked to Joe.

"So, by what you have confessed, we now know without a doubt that this is the son of God brought forth by immaculate conception! Our fellow scholars have searched far and wide for a baby said to have been born under a bright passing star. I take it you are the husband?"

"Well, er, yes?" That was all Joe could say.

"Were you present during the birth of the child?"

"Yes, I was. Myriam delivered the baby in a stable not far from here. There was this nasty innkeeper…" Here, the wise man interrupted. Joe noticed by the looks on their faces a sudden anxiety.

"Was there a bright star present above you during the birth?"

"Why, yes, there was. It seemed to scare the heck out of people all around these parts. I, however…"

"Joe!" Myriam exclaimed, trying to stop her husband from resorting to his blue-collar rhetoric. Jesus, startled by Myriam's voice, started to cry.

"Sorry, Myriam," Joe said after realizing his foul language was unsuitable for such visitors.

"Then you must listen closely to what we have to say. While searching for you, we met King Herod, Judea's ruler. His spies told him of the prophecy, and he asked that the newborn be brought to his palace once we found you. Beware, it is a trap. He considers the child a threat to his kingdom and has ordered all newborns in the area to be sought out and killed to stop the prophecy from coming true."

"Prophecy? What is the prophecy?" Joe asked, confused by all that was going on.

"This child, brought to earth by God, will become the King of Judea."

"What?" Joe said in disbelief. He had gone along with Myriam's story to appease his wife, but now, coming from such scholarly and wealthy men, he could not believe what was being said.

As Joe looked around, he saw many neighbors gathered around, listening and watching what was happening. Some were astonished at the words being spoken. Some even started to pray and worship the child from a distance. But others were also watching intently, their eyes on the gifts glittering in the setting sun. He could only imagine what they might do, for a profit or reward, if they could reach the local Roman authorities and provide such valuable information to Herod.

The wise men watched Joe's expression and seemed to read his mind. He was a husband, thinking only about the family's safety; the eyes focused on the crowd, not the gifts.

"You must flee from Judea immediately!" Melchior exclaimed. "The son of God is considered a threat to the Romans." Then, in a whisper, Melchior explained that one of his guards would assist them in their escape until they were safe from prying eyes and ears. Joe lost no time in gathering their things. Luckily, there were few possessions because he wanted to return to Nazareth someday. His only regret was leaving behind a rocking cradle he had made. Myriam was very proud of the quality and attention to detail.

In a field nearby, far away from prying eyes, Joe got the donkey ready to travel again. He carefully wrapped the precious items and packed them next to his tools in the hidden backrest of the donkey's saddle. In the evening, when it was dark and the stars filled the sky, Myriam and Joe were led away from Bethlehem, the destination to be revealed when they were far away from town.

Chapter 11

Far into the night and most of the next day, the guide led them south until they came upon a caravan heading to Egypt. Here, the guide bid them farewell and suggested they travel discreetly. Up to this point, Myriam had been very open about who Jesus was, but after hearing what Herod intended to do to her son, she took Joe's advice and kept the boy's identity a secret.

"Let's just say we found the child abandoned in the event anyone asks. Just until we get far enough away from Judea?" Joe pleaded as he walked beside the donkey while Myriam held the boy in her arms. Fortunately, they had little to fear because the caravan only cared about one thing: getting to Egypt without incident. They accepted the additions to the caravan gratefully, for in the desert, there is safety in numbers.

As the days passed, settlements and dwellings became scarce, and boredom set in. The scenery changed very little except for an occasional wadi that was usually dry. The camels, after centuries of walking the same paths as their ancestors, knew instinctively where the water holes were along the ancient trail. In the daytime, the desert wind would steal the moisture from your breath, so talking was minimal. The nights were bitter cold due to the lack of fuel to make a fire.

One day, while feeding the baby astride the donkey, Myriam's bare foot protruded from under her wraps. After days of monotony, Joe looked at the little foot and, with a mischievous smile, lifted his staff and touched her heel gently. Myriam flinched but kept on feeding. She was too busy keeping her balance to look down and see what touched her foot. Joe's smile turned into a big grin, and he touched the foot again, making Myriam flinch. The third time he tried it, Myriam almost lost her balance. Looking down, she gave a look that only a guilty husband can comprehend. He looked away and waited for her to speak.

"Joe, do that again, and that staff will be shoved somewhere you will regret!" Myriam said, but as she turned her head away, he thought he noticed just the slightest smile on her face.

The rest of that day, Joe behaved, but under his keffiyeh, he silently chuckled. Myriam did have a bit of a temper, and like any husband who never learns from the first confrontation, he liked to test the limits of her patience.

After long, weary days of monotonous travel, the caravan started to break up, and many went their way. Small towns began to appear and were close to the journey's end. Then, one morning, Joe saw a strange mountain range through the desert haze. At first, he thought he was seeing things—a mirage, they called it—a vision from lack of thirst and heat, but he was not thirsty, and the morning was cold. He blinked several times, and the mountains were still there. The ancient Egyptian pyramids were coming into view, and he could not believe his eyes.

While living in Judea, Joe observed many new building techniques from the Romans. He learned about using the keystone in an arch to keep it from falling and the difference between marble and granite in strength. As he traveled closer to Cairo, he could not believe the triangular shapes were man-made, no matter what others in the caravan said.

"There is no way human beings could have made those mountains; they had to have been made by God himself," Joe said as they approached the city. Myriam looked at the pyramids in wonder and agreed with her husband. Structures that large must have been made from a greater unseen power from heaven above. The closer they got to the three mountains, the bigger they became. Neither spoke for the last few miles; they just stared in awe. The journey had ended, and they were relieved that no one had followed the caravan to try and take Jesus away. Finally, they were safe in Egypt. Joe began to get emotional. He had been so worried the last few days. At night, he hardly slept, and during the day, he constantly looked back, expecting to see a legion of soldiers marching toward them.

"Myriam, I am sorry for how I have behaved with all that has happened. From your unwavering faith in God as the boy's father to the visit from those men of learning, I could not believe your story. But now, looking at what is before us, if God can create such massive shapes, so vast and perfect out of stone, he can create a son in your womb!"

Myriam was only half listening as she stared at the grand spectacle before her. Deep down, she knew he needed something beyond comprehension, something tangible, to believe in her and Jesus. It didn't matter if these pyramids before them were made by the pharaohs; all that mattered was for Joe to start having a little faith in God.

Chapter 12

Per the advice of a few traders in the caravan who knew Cairo well from previous visits, Joe found a neighborhood that welcomed foreigners. He rented a basement dwelling in the city's Jewish quarter and immediately set out to find a job.

After wandering about Cairo for only a few hours, Joe found work on a construction project among the Coptic inhabitants. After just a few days, he was praised by the foreman for his willingness to work hard and for long hours. After several weeks of Joe mingling with other families in the city, he allowed Myriam and Jesus to come and visit his new friends and coworkers. The family was accepted for who they were: good, hard-working people and no one seemed to care about the child's nationality or where he came from.

Still, they were afraid of what might happen if someone found out that the King of Judea wanted Jesus, so Myriam kept her word, not to mention that the young boy was the son of God. As months passed, their lives finally had a sense of routine. Between working long days and enjoying a few beers in the evening with friends, Joe was content in Cairo. He was getting to know Myriam more, too, and found her to be a strong young woman, protective of her son, who eventually started taking his first steps.

"Well, I would have expected the son of God just to stand up and start running," Joe said one evening when Jesus stood up on his own, smiled, took a few steps, and then fell flat on his face. Myriam instinctively rushed over to the boy, but Joe stopped her.

"Give him a second, and don't look worried; otherwise, he will think something is wrong and start to cry."

Jesus looked up and was about to start crying, but when he met Joe's smile, he paused, got up on hands and knees, stood up straight, wavered, and started walking straight toward Joe.

"Come on, kid," Joe said, holding his arms out straight. "You can do it, just a few more steps." Then Jesus made a final reach and almost fell, but Joe was there to catch him quickly.

"Gotcha!" Joe said and lifted the boy high into the air. Jesus laughed as he was twirled around in circles. Myriam watched and smiled while folding some clean work clothes. She was so happy that Joe accepted Jesus into the family; the first few months had been very trying, just like any newlyweds raising their first child. She was also amazed at how good a parent he was. Watching Joe so easily lift the boy into the air, she noticed his powerful biceps and thought he was not that bad-looking either, for an older man.

When Jesus had been worn out in play, the child immediately fell asleep, just like Joe said he would.

"Got to keep them moving; otherwise, they will cry all night," Joe said as he kicked up his feet and poured himself another beer from a large clay pot stored in a pit under the fireplace to keep the beverage cool.

"How many of those have you had?" Myriam asked. Joe was red in the face and seemed out of breath.

"Not enough to keep you from asking me," was the reply, followed by that mischievous grin that Myriam began to learn was his way of being provocative. "Why not have one yourself?"

"Certainly not! It would turn my milk sour probably and hurt the baby."

"Well, a beer just might make the boy sleep through the night, just a suggestion. Anyway, this stuff is much better than wine after a hard day on the job."

"Joe!" Myriam said while throwing a wrapped-up diaper at him. Thinking it was soiled, he ducked and then laughed when he found it was a ruse. Then he handed the clean diaper back, and she held his hand.

"What's this one from?" she asked, pointing to a scar inside the palm of his hand.

"Oh, that?" Joe said casually, with a touch of pride in his voice. Like any man, he relished talking about old wounds. "Years ago, I tripped on a board during a construction project, and my hand landed on a nail; it went right through." Myriam winced at the thought of a nail piercing one's hand that way.

"Did it hurt?" she asked while tenderly moving a finger over the scar. She was amazed at how such powerful, strong hands could be so gentle with the child.

"Sure, but luckily, it pierced this area of my hand and caused no issues. When it came out, I could keep working with a bandage tightly wound around it."

"You went back to work the next day?"

"Next day? I went back to work immediately! Dad said suck it up; construction does not wait for anybody. The stories I could tell you of mashed toes, broken bones, bad burns. Builders shake it off and keep working through an injury to support their families."

"Joe," Myriam said while still holding his hand.

"Yes?"

"It has been a few months since the birth, I mean. Have you thought about us at all now that we are safe?" Joe was taken aback. Of all the questions she could have asked, this was the last one he would have guessed. Myriam was now a young married woman, no longer a child. He decided to think carefully before saying anything that might hurt her feelings. As an older, active, hardworking man, Joe was content to come home, have a few beers, play with the child, and go to bed. Now, this was personal, and he dreaded saying the wrong thing.

"Of course, Myriam. But you know, having the child in jeopardy and all makes me believe we should be careful. Remember how difficult it was traveling with a baby on the donkey?"

"How could I forget? That dreadful animal seemed to want to throw me every chance, and you didn't help either. I remember that staff tickling my foot."

"Like any man, keep us from work, and we get into trouble."

"So, it isn't, it's not me?" Myriam asked, looking into his blue eyes. She was fascinated by them. In those eyes were wisdom and strength, which a mother depended upon to feel safe and secure.

"Are you kidding?" Joe said, taking her arm and turning it until she fell in his lap. You are the cutest girl in Egypt. Mummies would come back to life with just one look at you!"

"Oh, Joe!"

"Seriously, now, if you don't mind, one more beer before bed, please," he said while bumping her upright with his knee and then giving her backside a good smack.

"Okay, just one more, then we go to bed?" Myriam pleaded.

"Then to bed," he echoed with that mischievous grin as Joe drank the last beer of the day. Myriam smiled back. Like any young newly-wed, she hoped and prayed nothing was wrong with their relationship.

Chapter 13

As years passed, Joe reveled in each mishap, bump, and bruise the son of God inflicted upon himself. The kid was human, that was certain, and therefore easier to accept. From the patience of Myriam during potty training to the baby's first word, it was a joy to watch an infant go through the trials of childhood again, even if the kid wasn't his. The boy was good to his mother and obedient to his uncle Joe.

No matter how often Myriam tried to convince Joe that Jesus should call him "Dad," Joe refused, but he was a good father figure to Jesus and ensured the child respected his mom.

On a hot summer day, with temperatures well over one hundred degrees, Joe sat with some friends in a narrow, shaded alley, trying to keep cool during a work break. There, he overheard some merchant traders who traveled often to the north saying that Herod, King of Judea, had died. There was much speculation regarding his replacement and what new laws and regulations would be instituted to affect their profit margins.

Joe listened intently, and after asking around to make sure it was not some trap, he realized the boy was finally safe from danger. Though happy and content living in Egypt, Joe was ready to go home to the more temperate climate of Judea.

Myriam listened intently to the news and suggested that Joe speak to travelers coming from the north to make sure. Joe rode the donkey out of town, and the first caravan he came across verified the rumor was true. Herod was dead.

Jesus was a young boy now, happy and content among the Egyptians. When he was told it was time to return to their homeland, he got very emotional and had a temper tantrum. It took a long time to explain to the child why they would move. Finally, the boy calmed down. After the outburst, Joe realized how similar the boy was to his mother's temperament. Like anyone who has so many friends and each day is a joy, the prospect of having to leave for no apparent reason is hard to comprehend. Joe felt terrible and considered staying for good, but something told him this would not happen. Deep within was this ominous feeling that if they returned, regardless of the king's death, something terrible would happen. He discussed this with Myriam, and she had a similar feeling. Then she told Joe that it must be so; the future cannot be changed, and Jesus must return to Judea. When Joe asked why, Myriam said, "God commands it."

"Have you told the boy anything about his... Father?" Joe asked the night before departure.

"No, you asked me not to, and truthfully, I wish we could stay in Egypt. You are so happy with your friends and beer, but this is not our decision."

"God's then?"

"Yes."

"Myriam, I must admit that I have not believed any of this since the first day you told me by the fountain. Then, the wise men came, and

I still had difficulty believing. Watching Jesus play with other kids or greet strangers, I see something pure and good that can't be explained."

"Yes, I see it too. It's God speaking through his son. You see it in their faces, the joy of just being around him. That is why Jesus is so upset to leave; he feels the love of others around us."

"Why don't we just stay?"

"Because he must do what needs to be done."

"And that is?"

"We will just have to find out for ourselves."

"Myriam."

"Yes, Joe?"

"Can you just not tell Jesus who the actual, alleged, you know, who the real Father is?"

"I don't think I have to, Joe. Just watch him interact with others. Every action is pure good. He won't properly conceal himself during hide-and-seek so the other kids can quickly find him." The boy thinks of others before himself.

"Do you think he knows, then? Did he say something to that effect?" Joe asked in a surprised tone of voice.

"No, but a mother can always tell," Myriam answered.

"Okay, it's settled then. We leave tomorrow," Joe replied while blowing out the oil lamp and going to bed. He was so nervous about the journey that he snored all night. Myriam cradled and rocked Jesus until the child fell asleep. Then Myriam stayed up all night, brooding over how easy it was to extinguish the oil lamp and turn light into darkness. The action seemed significant somehow, as if it had a hidden meaning.

After many goodbyes and a promise to return one day to visit, the family joined a caravan north. Joe walked as usual, staff in hand, while Myriam and the boy rode on the donkey. Joe had suggested purchasing a camel, but Myriam said there was no need. Joe made some new modifications to the saddle to accommodate mother and child, and after her nod of approval, it was time to go home after years in exile.

Jesus was at an age when a child's brain was addicted to learning. To get the boy interested in the journey, Joe decided to go north to Alexandria first before heading back to Judea. He was told of a library there with scholars who could tutor Jesus on many subjects. Also, several friends in Cairo who had been to Alexandria spoke of this vast body of salt water with enormous fish, which were said to be very tasty if you could catch them.

Upon arrival in Alexandria, Jesus enjoyed the library so much that Joe extended the stay and fished in the Great Sea while Myriam stayed with the boy during lessons. The scholars in the library marveled at how quickly Jesus learned. They showed Jesus scrolls and stone tablets from different languages and explained the story of Moses and his journey to the promised land.

When it was time to leave, Jesus was thankful Uncle Joe had brought him to Alexandria. The boy apologized to Uncle Joe and his mother for his outburst and said he would try to control his temper in the future.

Joe welled up from the earnest apology. He was getting very attached to this "Son of God." He wished they could stay in Alexandria, especially now that he had tasted saltwater fish, but Myriam was insistent. It was time to go home.

The journey east was uneventful, as the caravan they attached to was very big. There was no sign of Roman soldiers or fear of bandits, just a vast desert and dry wadi as far as the eye could see. Occasionally, in rocky areas, the trail had a faint white color of bleached bones from dead camels (and some humans) who had been ground into dust over hundreds of years along this ancient trade route.

When they reached Wadi Ghazza, the river many considered the dividing line between Palestine and Egypt, Joe's heart sank, but he did not know why. During the rest of the journey, Myriam remained silent, keeping her thoughts to herself.

Jesus, however, was in high spirits and insisted on walking next to his uncle that day. After a few hours, the fast pace and the heat of the day got the better of him.

"Carry me?" Jesus asked.

"No, I will not carry you for the rest of the day. Back up on the donkey with your mother," Joe replied.

"Just for a little bit, please?"

"Oh, alright. Myriam, hold the staff. Up you go on my shoulders."

Once Joe had the boy on his back, he regretted the decision because the boy was growing fast, and the trail was not very level.

"Why are those men picking up the camel poops?" Jesus asked while watching some old Arabs pick up fresh dung that had dropped onto the trail.

"They will use that for fuel to cook. When you live in the desert, nothing goes to waste."

"Can I help?" Jesus asked.

"Ask your mother," Joe said with a mischievous smile.

"Joe, wipe that smile off your face, or I will do it with this staff!" Jesus had learned from his mother's tone when she was kidding and when she was serious. This time, he was not sure. Uncle Joe had said something to get his mom aroused, but he did not understand why. Without saying anything else, Joe places Jesus back on the donkey, takes his staff, and keeps walking with a smile. That was the first time since they had left Alexandria that he got Myriam aroused, but after several hours of silence afterward, he got the impression something was wrong with his wife.

"You alright, Myriam?" Joe asked after Jesus, exhausted from walking, finally fell asleep in her arms.

"I'm okay. I'm just thinking about going back; that's all."

"What do you say we spend a few days in Hebron first and get some information regarding Nazareth?" Joe asked. Somehow, he was in no great hurry to get back home. Myriam seemed to feel the same way.

"That's fine with me."

In Hebron, the family said goodbye to the caravan and found a place to stay for a few days. Joe found some work to keep busy and pay for the travel expenditures. Myriam spent her days with Jesus, keeping a close eye on the boy as any concerned parent would in a strange town.

Eventually, the typical nosy neighbors would find an excuse to stop by and ask questions about the boy's origin. Myriam just shrugged and asked why it mattered. Then Jesus would look into their eyes and smile. The child's presence was contagious, and everyone in the surrounding area soon wanted to be near the boy. There was an aura about him, and it felt good. Strangely, this made Myriam both proud and yet, for some reason, afraid. For Joe, it was perfect for business. People started to hire him, anticipating meeting this Black child from some distant land. The prestige felt good and became a novelty, but Myriam didn't like it. Eventually, she decided it was time to make the final journey home and started thinking about her friends and family. Would they be as happy to meet her son for the first time as everyone else?

Chapter 14

As Passover approached, Judea was crammed with pilgrims. Lodgings were hard to come by, as were the sacrificial animals presented to God according to ancient custom. The city of Nazareth was no exception, and the prices for everything were exorbitant, according to the old law of supply and demand. For Joe and any modest family, spending money was monitored carefully.

"You have to get a lamb," Myriam said to Joe.

"Why can't I just capture some pigeons like last time?" Joe interjected. He knew Myriam was insistent that Jesus be brought up in strict accordance with the Torah.

"This is our first Passover since we left Egypt, and I want to make an actual sacrifice, even if you think it costs too much."

"The priests always get the best parts of the animals, I was just—"

"Joseph, son of Jacob, get the lamb!" Myriam said defiantly.

"Yes, Myriam," Joe said, sulking out of the house. He knew the argument was over once she spoke in that formal tone. As he left, Joe muttered quietly, "Our ancestors fled the Pharaohs to a promised land. Now I wish we were back there."

"I heard that!" Myriam shouted through the door.

"Can I come along, Uncle Joe?" Jesus asked.

"Ask your mother."

"Can I, Mom?"

"Yes, but don't wander off in the market. It is so busy this time of year."

"I won't. Where are we going?" Jesus asked, taking his uncle's hand before entering the crowded street.

"We are off to get a sacrificial lamb … or maybe a kid," Joe said with that mischievous grin.

"A kid?" Jesus asked. Then, after pondering for a moment, he asked, "They sacrifice kids?"

"Sure, when kids are bad and kick their elders, we sacrifice them to teach the other kids a lesson."

"But I am a kid!" Jesus said with a look of surprise.

"True, so you better be good at the market; otherwise…"

"Joe, keep it up, and you are going to be sacrificed!" Myriam said, peering out the doorway.

"Okay, okay, we are going," Joe replied, the grin turning into a smile. Myriam smiled in return before going back inside. As they walked to the market, Jesus remained on his best behavior, and Joe, thinking he had done the boy a practical pleasantry, walked happily with the boy as they navigated the crowded streets. In a way, it felt good to have tricked the Son of God, Joe thought to himself.

At the market, Joe found a vendor selling lambs and goats.

"So, shall we sacrifice a lamb or a kid?" Joe asked, trying to scare Jesus again now that Myriam was no longer around to interject.

"You don't like the taste of goat, remember?" Jesus said, mimicking Joe's mischievous grin.

"Lamb it is," Joe said after a pause. His face went from surprise to disappointment, to wonder, then joy. It was Joe who had been tricked by Jesus, and he was proud. If he had taught the boy anything, it was humor. When they had reached a vendor selling lambs, the proprietor looked at Joe and then at the boy, trying to size them up. Seeing the child was Black, he assumed the child was the man's slave. Both looked well off with clean clothes and new sandals.

"We need a lamb," Joe said to the owner.

"Only have this one left," the proprietor said. The lamb looked sick and was bleating for milk.

"How much?" Joe asked. He didn't care about the condition of the animal, for he knew the priests would take most of the meat. If this lamb could be gotten for a good price, he would save money.

"Like I said, last one. Fifteen shekels," the proprietor said. Joe winced. The lamb wasn't worth half that price. Since they were new to the area, Joe had not been able to walk around and compare prices. With the Passover at hand, Myriam insisted a lamb be purchased today. Joe was just about to make a counteroffer when Jesus spoke.

"Poor little lamb pines for its mother and is hungry too. My Father demands a lamb without blemish, like the one you have in the pen out back. That one we will sacrifice, and this one will grow up to reproduce as it should be."

As the boy spoke, Joe and the proprietor looked at each other in shame. In their minds, they were both trying to profit from a holy sacrifice, and this boy seemed to subtly call them out on what they were doing; just like a parent teaches a child how to behave properly through example, Jesus was teaching them to be honest with each other.

"I have a lamb out back that you can have for ten shekels," the proprietor said to Joe.

"Ten is a fair price. I will take it," Joe replied mechanically. He suddenly felt it was not right to haggle while Jesus was there. A few minutes later, the proprietor came back with a pure white lamb, healthy and worthy of sacrifice.

On the way home, Jesus led the animal on a rope, and the lamb obediently followed as if proud to have been chosen. Joe walked behind the boy and pondered Jesus' words: "My Father demands a lamb without blemish." Was the boy referring to Joe or God when he spoke to the proprietor? After the Passover, Joe told Myriam what had transpired at the market and how Jesus reacted.

"I felt as though he saw right through me, and the salesman seemed to feel the same way—ashamed. Myriam, please be honest. Did you finally tell the boy who his Father allegedly is?" Joe asked, looking into Myriam's eyes. She didn't answer, didn't have to; she looked just as astonished as he did.

That was the last time Joe played any pranks on Jesus.

Chapter 15

A s years passed, Jesus worked in the family trade. Joe marveled at how easily the young man learned techniques that had taken him years to master. Jobs that would take Joe a day to complete, Jesus could finish in half the time. Joe was proud when Jesus presented a drinking cup carved out of a solid block of olive wood as the final project for his rite of passage to journeyman carpenter. Joe suggested that wherever Jesus traveled, he should bring the cup along to show prospective customers his skill as a craftsman.

When the work was completed for the day, Jesus would spend time with his group of friends known as the disciples. Some of these people seemed to be nothing more than freeloaders to Joe, and he was concerned that Jesus spent his money a little too freely on this motley crew. With the gifts given by the Magi and his share in the business, Jesus was quite wealthy for his social status, but he did not flaunt or act like a rich person. Instead, Jesus was generous but not foolish. His wages, after providing for his mom, were given to those in need.

As Jesus grew into a man, word spread about his wisdom, and people would gather to hear him speak. Eventually, the crowds made it hard for the family to have a normal life. To Joe, a hardworking man who liked to keep to himself, the celebrity status was too much. Eventually, he would pack up and move the family to another town.

When Myriam asked the reason for moving, he just said a carpenter's family must go where the work is. Jesus didn't complain and seemed to enjoy the itinerant lifestyle. It was as if he wanted to visit as many people as possible.

The family eventually migrated north to Joe's favorite area of Galilee. Here, Joe felt at home. Being a rural area, there was not much work, but there were not many people either. When there was a lull in work, Joe took up his favorite pastime of fishing in the Sea of Chinnereth. He would usually go alone and return with fresh fish. During this time of solitude, Joe would think back to his former life and family. As he explored the shoreline, he tried to remember the exact location of the hidden underwater pier he constructed decades ago. After searching for several days, he finally gave up. The memory was the past, gone, and so was the family he once had. Joe realized then that you just can't relive the life you once had.

Chapter 16

During this time, there was a Nazirite prophet known as John the Baptist who traveled about preaching that God was watching and would judge those who did not repent for their sins. This man led a strict life of poverty and abstinence, wore only simple clothes, and provided sustenance by foraging for food in the wild. While Joe was away fishing, Jesus and Mary happened to meet John while the man was providing a baptism in the River Jordan. It was a typical sunny and hot day, and the river was like an oasis with trees growing on the banks that provided shade while the cool water was a relief to the weary.

In the river, by a cutout that led to a sandbank, they watched John perform the ceremony of baptism for a small group gathered around the sandbank.

John would take a person in his arms and gently lower the body into the river while asking God to forgive the sinner who was now ready to repent. When the sinner finished with the baptism, they walked out of the water feeling refreshed and clean, and Jesus noticed that each one left the water with a smile and looked relieved.

"Let's go down to the water's edge and cool off," Mary suggested, and as they approached, Jesus became more interested in what John was doing.

"He speaks of God and the removal of sins through repentance. All from taking a dip in that wonderful cool water," Jesus said while watching another person being baptized.

"He may be speaking the words of God, but I'm not going into the middle of the river to be drowned; I can't swim," Mary said while removing her sandals and stepping ankle-deep into the river. The sand had a fine texture and felt good between the toes, and there were no sharp rocks.

"I would like to go in the water, Mother," Jesus said as his interest grew in the words John was preaching.

"No, you won't; you will drown. That water is deep where that man is standing."

While the two were arguing, John approached and was upon them before they had finished.

"You need not worry, Mother; I will hold your son under just long enough for him to be cleansed. Trust in God, and he will be free from all sins, that is, if he believes," John said.

The sudden approach of John had startled Mary, and she stared at the man before speaking. He was soaking wet, wearing only a loincloth made of animal skin. His long hair was disheveled, and his body was so thin that he looked like a skeleton come to life. Yet, as she looked into the man's brown eyes, she noticed something similar in appearance to her son. He seemed to look right through her, guessing her thoughts. She looked away, embarrassed, and was about to suggest to Jesus that they leave when she noticed that John was leading him toward the river.

"Are you a sinner?" John asked just before they reached the water's edge. Here, Mary was about to protest, not for Jesus being led into the river but for the question asked of her son, the Son of God Himself. As if reading her thoughts, Jesus looked at his mother while answering.

"What is considered to be a sin in the eyes of God?" Jesus asked.

"An excellent question. May I please ask your name?" John answered.

"My name is Jesus, and this is my mother, Mary. Please tell me, why should I be baptized?" Jesus said.

"One question at a time. A sin is when you stray away from God's will to do what is right. The path to damnation starts with committing just one sin. Once you accept that sin as okay, you open the possibility to more sins until there is no turning back. Through this baptism, if you are sorry for what you have done, God will forgive you. But beware, just going through the ceremony and not truly being repentant for what you have done, God will know. Therefore, confess only what you plan to correct and leave what you struggle with inside until the day comes when you are ready to ask for your Father's forgiveness."

Here, Mary caught her breath. Could this man know who Jesus's father is? Before she could say anything, Jesus spoke.

"I have a temper that I inherited from my mother." Here, Mary turned red as the evening sun, but the feeling of embarrassment quickly passed when she saw that mischievous grin on Jesus's face, which was similar to her husband's.

"Everyone has a temper; it is human nature," John replied while looking at Mary. Then he spoke to both of them in unison.

"Has this temper caused thoughts or actions that would not please God?"

"Maybe," Jesus replied. "But I have not yet had the pleasure to meet God and ask him." At first, Mary thought that John was going to be cross with Jesus for speaking about God in such a lighthearted manner, but he replied,

"Well said. Only God can read your thoughts, especially those that happened long ago. Tell me, has your temper ever caused your mother to not be pleased?"

"Absolutely," Jesus replied with sincerity while looking over to his mother.

"Then, in the eyes of God, you have sinned because God expects you to honor your mother if she is doing her best to bring you up in this world."

"She always has. I have sinned and am ready to repent," Jesus said as John lowered the body into the River Jordan.

When Jesus rose and stepped onto the shore, Mary noticed a change in her son. He was smiling, yet not in a way that bestowed happiness. It was a smile of relief as if a huge weight was lifted from her son. Jesus then walked directly over to his mom and, still dripping with water, gave her a hug and apologized for all the times he threw a temper tantrum when he was a little boy in Egypt. Mary was so overwhelmed by her son's actions that she ignored being soaked and hugged her son back. Jesus then thanked Mary for raising him from a boy into a man.

John moved on to the next person and took no further notice of the Black young man accompanied by a white mother. It was as if he knew who this young man's true Father was and why he came to the river at this time. As Jesus and Mary walked away John paused and watched them leave. He knew that a temper is not a sin but an action, like eating or drinking, and can resurface at any time if someone is not careful.

Chapter 17

After the baptism, Jesus changed. He felt a new purpose to spread God's word and devoted much of his time speaking in the temple. Many came and asked him questions on various topics and were amazed by his vast knowledge, especially of history. Jesus taught those who would listen that civilizations were like the lifecycle of man. From childhood, we are innocent until pride, anger, greed, vanity, or lust take hold and corrupt the towns and peoples. Then, old age and darkness ensues, the foundations crumble into dust to be used as bricks for the next generation to learn from their mistakes or repeat the history lesson through ignorance.

When Jesus entered a new town and began to preach, crowds appeared in greater numbers to listen. Myriam was pleased, albeit secretly frightened of her son's increasing celebrity. Still, nothing bad had happened, and the smiles on everyone's faces who followed Jesus made her a proud mother. Joe was pleased, too; the biological bond between mother and son was obvious, and they were both young. His job as guardian was just about complete. Jesus was a man now and capable of taking care of himself and his mom. Joe started to feel like an outsider, and the age gap did not help. Gradually, he distanced himself when

Myriam and Jesus traveled about. He would use the excuse that he had work to finish, and over time, he watched as Jesus's popularity grew and the mother's pride along with it.

Now that Jesus was a man, Joe had no hard feelings about the boy leaving work as a carpenter to become a preacher. Besides, Joe thought, once you learned a trade, you can always go back. The boy had worked hard and accumulated enough money to work when he wanted to. What irritated Joe the disciples who were growing in number and always seemed to be there whenever Jesus began to preach. To Joe, he wondered what they did for a living and whether any of them had jobs. They were, however, a comfort in terms of protection, for bandits rarely attacked a large group. If anything, they gave him comfort, knowing Myriam and Jesus were safe wherever they traveled.

Myriam had a friend, Noa, who had little money and practically spent her life savings on her daughter's wedding reception.

As with any wedding invitations, it was expected the husband and wife should attend, but for Joe, now in his sixties, the thought of being in a room full of kids having kids was not appealing, so he asked Jesus to take his place.

When Jesus and Myriam arrived at the wedding, her friend was a bit taken aback by meeting Jesus for the first time. Myriam was about to explain her immaculate conception when the manager of the banquet interrupted them. Noa had purchased five jugs of wine paid for in advance, but as the jugs were brought forth for the celebration, they were half the size of a normal wine cask. Noa pleaded with the manager, but he just replied, "You haggled for five jugs of wine, and this is what you get. If you are not satisfied, then you can get more wine from the shop across the street."

"Jesus, is there something you can do to assist?" Myriam asked.

Now, the manager had an agreement with the wine shop and had played this ruse before with other desperate patrons.

"What is in those jugs against the wall?" Jesus asked, pointing to five large jars inside the entrance hallway. The manager turned red and then, after thinking for a while, replied with a smile.

"Those are filled with water," the manager said.

"Then we will have water mixed with wine for the celebration."

When Noa heard about this, she sighed and agreed. After all, they were there to celebrate two young people in love. The manager relented and sent for the jugs to be brought over. When the waiters poured the water, the wedding guests gasped in astonishment; the water had turned into wine. For the rest of the evening, everyone drank their fill, astonished by the miracle Jesus had performed. He was the party's highlight, and Myriam was so pleased until some elders forbade Jesus from mingling with their fair-skinned daughters. Myriam left the wedding very sad but kept it to herself. She realized her son was different but thought her friends would accept him as they had accepted her. From that day forward, she distanced herself from those who did not respect Jesus for what he was: a good and decent person. Jesus never forgot how his mother was treated. From that day forward, he sought out only those who truly needed God's love—the destitute, sick, homeless, prostitutes, slaves, and criminals who had no one and were shunned or ignored by society.

Chapter 18

†

After Jesus preached to the crowds, a few individuals stayed behind, hoping to speak to Jesus in person. One of those was a beggar who called out after everyone had dispersed.

"Please help a blind man with a shekel?" the man said to Jesus just as he was about to leave. Jesus looked over at the man, then he approached and stooped down so no one could hear their conversation.

"Are you happy being a blind beggar?"

No one had ever asked him anything before, and the man thought about this question for a long time before replying.

"No, I am not," the beggar said dejectedly.

"What would you like to do?" Jesus asked.

The beggar could not believe it. Someone seemed to care about him. Without hesitation, he answered.

"I would like to be a shepherd. I have always enjoyed being in the company of animals, but one day, I was desperate and decided to play on the sympathy of others. Now, I am known as the blind beggar, and no one will hire me for anything."

"Would you like my help?" Jesus asked.

"Yes, please. If I could stop being this blind beggar, I would be eternally grateful."

The disciples witnessed from a distance as Jesus touched the beggar's eyes and then asked the man to stand up. At this point, a crowd and the disciples gathered to see what was happening.

"Rise and be a blind beggar no more," Jesus said. Then he spoke to the crowd. "This man is no longer blind and is good with sheep. Is there anyone who would give him a job so he no longer has to beg to feed his family?" Out of the crowd, a nobleman stepped forward.

"I have a flock this man can tend if he truly can now see," the man said with doubt.

"I promise to watch over your flock night and day if you will give me a chance to prove myself," the beggar said. Then, he thanked Jesus for this second chance. The crowd that had gathered around was amazed. Jesus had turned a blind beggar into a good shepherd.

Chapter 19

Mariam was increasingly pleased by her son's good deeds but also began to feel troubled. Since leaving Egypt, a feeling of dread had been growing inside her—it was a mother's intuition. The young man was so knowledgeable about many topics that he often debated in the temple with scholars who were amazed by his vast knowledge yet not ready to have someone so young, not to mention Black, tell them what was right or just. While preaching, Jesus stated that God was his father, and people interpreted this metaphorically. Mariam was relieved because this removed the need for the explanation of his biological father that she kept secret as a promise to Joe. She often wondered if Jesus knew about the prophecy foretold long ago but did not ask.

As time passed, Mariam still traveled with Jesus and kept to the perimeter of the crowds, listening to discussions about her son while he preached. As Jesus's popularity grew, the talks about him began to be mixed. Many priests in the temple were not pleased with some of the ideals Jesus spoke against, particularly God's expectation for everyone to assist those in need. Mariam also noted that not all in the crowd wanted spiritual healing; many just wanted to see this Son of God for themselves in the hopes of witnessing some miracle. Others thought that if Jesus were to touch them, wealth and prosperity would surely follow.

At home, Mariam turned to Joe, and they discussed her concerns.

"He is his own man now; there is nothing I can say or do to change that," Joe said one evening while cleaning his tools in the soft yellow light of an oil lamp. He had also listened to some of the conversations in the crowds that gathered to hear Jesus speak and was of the same opinion that feelings about Jesus and his preaching were beginning to be mixed. Some people were actually starting to think that Jesus was a little above himself.

"I know, Joe, but that dreadful feeling that something bad will happen won't go away," Mary replied.

"Yeah, I am beginning to get the same feeling. I was there at his last preaching, though you did not see me. I listened to the conversations in the crowd, and not all were positive. Some predicted that Jesus would soon be a high priest and expect sacrifices in his honor, while others said he was an agent of Rome and spoke like a typical publican."

"What can be done, Joe? I am worried about my son," Mariam said.

"Nothing can be undone; that is the real problem. Jesus is now preaching more than teaching, and if there is one thing that gets people upset, it's being told what to do," Joe exclaimed.

"Can you speak to him?" Mariam pleaded.

"He is not my son, remember? Besides, I believe his real Father is beginning to speak through him," Joe said flatly as he picked up a chisel and began honing the edge against a soft stone. They were silent for the rest of the evening, each thinking about the prophecy the wise men foretold and what it meant for Jesus and his future. That evening, Joe sat up long into the night worrying like any concerned parent until their child came home safe.

Chapter 20

While Jesus traveled with the disciples, John the Baptist was arrested and imprisoned for speaking out against the new King of Judea for breaking the Jewish law that forbade marrying his brother's wife, who was divorced.

Hitherto, Roman officials ignored John due to his hermit lifestyle. To Herod Antipas, John was eccentric, but some believed this man was the chosen one mentioned in the prophecy long ago. After Jesus's baptism, John the Baptist began to enter towns and cities, preaching publicly and stating that it was time for those who had sinned to be judged. No ruler in Rome would allow anyone to speak against the empire, even if John's statement about breaking Jewish law were accurate. The king was Roman and had no mind for local religious rites.

"How dare you speak openly against my desires?" the king's wife told John when he was brought before the court bound in chains.

"I only speak what is right and just. But it does not matter anymore, for the one that was foretold has come. The son of God will pass judgment in my defense."

"Who is this other person you speak of?" the King asked. He was not pleased to hear that there was another prophet to worry about. His agents had always thought that John the Baptist was the chosen one spoken of in the prophecy years ago.

"Someone I am not worthy to wash the dirt from his sandals," John replied as he looked around the court and met everyone's gaze. Many there looked away in shame except one, the king's wife.

"Herod, you are King of Judea; no one is greater than you. Will you sit here and take this insult?"

The King knew she was right; he could not just sit here and let this man insult his family.

"Take him away," Herod said with hesitation, for there was much social unrest throughout Judea, and this John was looked upon as a holy man among the Essenes, a faction known to preach the coming of a Messiah. The last thing Herod wanted was a riot when sympathizers found out John was imprisoned. Then there was this other man John spoke of; could this person be the so-called Messiah? Immediately, the king sent his agents to find this person John spoke of so he could be brought forth and questioned. If indeed this other man even existed.

Days later, during the King's birthday, his stepdaughter danced for the event. She was a captivating woman and wore fine, see-through silk that revealed her voluptuous body. As the music played, the King was aroused as she provocatively moved her hips and stomach. The erotic display not only pleased the men but even some of the women at the party.

There was much applause when the music was over, and the crowd asked the girl to dance again. After refusing many times, the King offered her anything she desired in exchange for just one more performance.

The stepdaughter was called aside by her mother, and after a brief conversation, the daughter smiled and asked in a loud voice for everyone to hear. "Give me the head of the one who so dared to speak against your marriage to my mother, and I will dance!"

She looked directly at Herod and waited for an answer. With one hand on her hip, she turned a leg to the side, opening the dress entirely and exposing her. The crowd cheered and demanded another dance.

Herod pondered for a moment. True, there might be potential rioting in the streets if word got out that John the Baptist was executed, but as he stared at such young flesh, he became even more aroused for his stepdaughter. With a heavy heart, the King sent word for the execution.

A short time later, while the party was still in progress, John's head was presented on a silver platter. The blood, still warm, pooled in a crimson circle as John's eyes looked into the crowd as if they could still see and judge. Many looked away in disgust, but when the head was brought before the stepdaughter, she grabbed the hair, held the head up, and stared triumphantly back into John's dead eyes for a long time. Then she gave the King a seductive glance, slapped John's face, and dropped the head onto the platter. Immediately, music started to play, and she danced, knowing the king had chosen her that evening over her mother.

Chapter 21

Jesus took after his mother in many aspects, one being short-tempered, especially with those who wronged others. His sense of good judgment in others came from Uncle Joe. The two men were so different, yet somehow, Myriam realized there was a reason why Joe was chosen to be their guardian and protector.

An example was Joe's ability to read a person as honest or deceitful, unlike Jesus, who always seemed to give everyone the benefit of the doubt. One instance was a huge gathering to hear Jesus preach in a rural area with very few shops to purchase food. When it came time to break the fast, a basket was passed around to collect food for the crowd, but it had only produced a few loaves of bread and a couple of fish.

Jesus spoke to the crowd and said that God would provide. Joe, who was present at the gathering, had another idea. He took a basket in hand and walked among the crowd for a second collection. When he approached someone with a heavy knapsack or bulging pockets, he would look into their eyes and nod to the basket in his hands. When Joe was finished walking among the crowd, there was enough food for everyone present, with excess given to the poor. The crowd was astonished and said it was a miracle. When Joe looked askance at Jesus, he said, "God has provided."

Joe noted many of the disciples as they became attached to Jesus. Some of these individuals were summoned personally, like Peter, a fisherman. When Joe heard how Jesus walked on water to approach Peter, he smiled but kept his thoughts and fond memories of the submerged pier to himself. Joe thought Peter was a born follower, easily persuaded yet loyal, who would always be at Jesus's side. Peter gave Joe a sense of security due to his massive frame from hauling in fishing nets all his life. As long as he was present, no robbers would attempt to attack Jesus. Joe eventually stopped staying up late worrying about Jesus for he knew Peter would ensure everyone was safe.

One disciple, however, called Matthew, seemed oddly familiar to Joe. Matthew reminded him of Barbee, and Joe wondered if the two knew each other. For instance, Matthew was a tax collector and kept to himself. Like Barbee, he always observed from a distance and kept his back to a wall. The difference between the two was that Matthew constantly took notes. Joe was wary of any publican but did not get the feeling Matthew would attempt anything sinister. Judas, however, was a disciple who was always there to assist and appease everyone. Joe never trusted Judas. Interestingly, Joe noticed that Matthew did not associate willingly with Judas either. To Joe, these disciples were a strange mix of characters, yet they all seemed devoted to Jesus somehow. Some of the devotion was obvious—they were following because they were lost and needed guidance. Others were there to be a part of a new and popular crowd. Regardless of their intentions, most of the disciples seemed loyal to Jesus—for now, Joe thought.

Then, a turn of events happened that got Jesus into trouble. He was walking along with his disciples when a young, neatly dressed boy approached, holding out his hand.

"Please, sir, may I have a shekel?" the boy asked, sizing up the crowd and smiling. Indeed, this celebrity with so many followers would gladly give a handout.

Jesus looked down upon the smiling child with hand extended.

"This boy is Want," Jesus said to the crowd. "Over there is Need." The crowd looked directly opposite the boy and saw a little girl dressed in rags, too scared to come out from under a vendor's cart. The boy looked over at the little girl with an angry expression. People always gave the little girl money. He would deal with her later, like he always did.

"Who should be given the shekel?" Jesus asked the crowd. Then, without glancing at the boy, Jesus started walking away. One of the disciples approached the girl and gave her two shekels. She smiled and thanked him for his kindness. As the crowd passed, the boy took out a rock that was polished as if handled often. He waited for the right moment and, quick as lightning, flicked the stone toward Jesus's head.

It was as if, by intuition, Jesus had moved aside, and the rock had passed unnoticed. Jesus kept walking without looking back as the boy stood motionless for some time, staring in astonishment. How could that man have known a stone was coming from behind? When the crowd was gone, the boy turned to face the girl; now, he thought, he would get his two shekels.

When the boy approached, the girl stood her ground. In her left hand was the money, and in her right hand was a rock. The boy ran away in fright to tell his father, a high priest, how Jesus had humiliated him, a high priest's son, in front of a crowd. The father of the boy had heard rumors of this Jesus for some time and from that day forward, the boy's father decided to have Jesus placed under surveillance.

Chapter 22

Jesus was observed to obey the strict laws and customs of the Jewish faith. What concerned the high priests was the fact Jesus was Black and obviously from some distant country far away. They wondered where his civilization was and if there were others just as wise with the knowledge of the world. Until now, Jesus was an upstanding citizen who paid his taxes and had no conflicts with church and state. But he had one flaw, and that was his temper. Shortly after the incident with the boy, Jesus went to preach in the temple as he had done so many times before. Jesus had previously stated that no money lending or street vendors should be allowed in such a sacred place, but his demands were never enforced. When Jesus returned to the temple unannounced, there were the same vendors. They scoffed at Jesus and taunted him. Who was this Black man giving orders? The vendors paid an exorbitant bribe to the high priests for this lucrative location. They could make a year's profit alone when the pilgrims flocked into the city for Passover.

"So, you have returned in complete disregard to the sanctity of God's house. Leave immediately," Jesus said, but they taunted Jesus instead.

"Who are you to tell us what to do?" they mocked.

Now, the disciples had gathered around, and they shouted in agreement. The temple was a sacred place meant for prayer, not commerce. Jesus was right, and the vendors needed to leave. As Jesus got angry, a crowd gathered and jeered him to take a stand and throw these vendors out.

Joe, who knew how quickly a crowd could turn into a mob, was not there to stop Jesus as he toppled over the tables and let loose the tethered animals that were for sale. In the excitement, the crowd fought for the stray coins. Many of the disciples fled in panic, with a few exceptions. Peter stayed by Jesus and protected him from the angry vendors, while Judas ran among the crowd, grabbing any stray coins. Matthew, from a distance, recorded the incident. The high priests had what they needed to get this disturber of the peace thrown in jail. Meanwhile, the vendors quickly notified some soldiers of the incident, and Peter convinced Jesus to leave just before the soldiers arrived.

As Jesus left the scene, he was approached by a man named Joseph of Arimathea. This man was a revered member of society who often listened to Jesus's teachings in the temple. He recommended that Jesus accompany him to his house until the riot dispersed.

Jesus was taken to Joseph's private library and shown many ancient scrolls of different languages collected over many years. When Jesus started to interpret the ancient texts, Joseph was convinced this man was different, someone to be listened to and not ridiculed.

"They are afraid of you, and for good reason. You know so much of the ancient past and are not swayed by money or politics," Joseph said as he showed Jesus an ancient text he did not understand.

"This is written in Coptic, an ancient civilization that still exists," Jesus said after interpreting a few words into Hebrew.

"They are only afraid because they control this ancient knowledge and want to keep it to themselves," Jesus replied while handing back the ancient text.

"But you could teach this knowledge, and many, including myself, would be willing to listen," Joseph said, handing Jesus other scrolls and texts from distant lands. Jesus was able to interpret them all, including Egyptian hieroglyphics.

"My time is coming to teach the world about righteousness and redemption," Jesus replied while picking up an old broken stone tablet. "This civilization, so long ago, worshiped their God through human sacrifice. Their priests performed the ritual to scare the parishioners into submission. The priests in the temple today are no better; they care only about themselves while they should be using their stature for humanitarian purposes."

"That outburst in the temple will get you thrown in prison or worse," Joseph said with a severe look.

"Indeed, just like the parents who opposed the sacrifice of their sons and daughters and spoke against this ancient religion," Jesus replied while staring at the stone tablet as if remembering something terrible and sad from the past. Jesus handed it back with a look of remorse on his face.

"You are not afraid of what they will do?" Joseph asked carefully. He was unsure if Jesus knew the Sanhedrin had already been gathering information against him after he humiliated the son of a high priest.

"John the Baptist was one such person executed for speaking against the priests and the rulers of Judea. There will be others after me who will bring judgment upon those who use power and persuasion to influence the weak. I know what is coming for me, and it cannot be stopped," Jesus said while peering into Joseph's eyes. Joseph turned away, ashamed. Yes, he was one of those who had done many things for his benefit, but now, after meeting with Jesus, he wanted to change.

"I can't do anything to persuade them otherwise," Joseph said.

"I know; that is why I came to visit you. Afterward, when my time has passed, you can assist the disciples in spreading the word of God to others."

"I will do what I can, Jesus," Joseph said. When Jesus left that evening, word had already reached the priests of what had transpired in the temple. One of them was the boy's father, whom Jesus had made an example of. The priests now had their case and immediately brought charges against Jesus. A warrant was issued for Jesus to be arrested for disturbing the peace, causing property damage, stealing, and disregarding the sanctity of the temple.

Chapter 23

Whenever Jesus and Myriam were away traveling, Joe's old habits came back. Dishes piled up in the kitchen, and he did not care about his appearance. In the evenings, he enjoyed sitting back with a jug of wine, watching the world go by, but without the family around, it was too quiet. He missed the sporadic bang or clatter from someone else in the home and admitted to himself that he was once again lonely.

By now, the family was doing quite well financially, and Joe worked only to keep busy. Being alone had some advantages. It was more relaxing not having the Son of God in the home. It is not that Jesus ever passed judgment, but it could be stressful to always be on his best behavior, especially when it came to the foul language.

After several weeks of being alone, Joe looked around and decided to clean up the kitchen. A vision of Myriam returning unannounced and seeing the mess was something he did not want. While he cleaned, Joe sang a working man's song containing profanity. Since no one was around, he gradually sang louder until a sudden knock at the door startled him.

An elderly woman needed her goat pen mended. Her husband had died the previous year, and now she was alone. Joe was embarrassed about being caught singing such vulgar words, but when the visitor turned out not to be his wife, he was so relieved that he decided to fix the pen at no charge.

The woman was so grateful that it made Joe feel good about doing charity work. Never in his life had he ever completed a job for free, that was not how he was brought up.

The next day, he set out to impoverished neighborhoods and started volunteering his labor to those who needed repairs. With each act of charity, Joe felt enlightened and the loneliness went away. Jesus, even when not present, was affecting Joe spiritually, and he was grateful.

As weeks passed and there was no sign of Jesus and Myriam, Joe became worried and decided to search for his family. The trail was not difficult to follow. Joe would enter a town, and there would be talk about Jesus and the good deeds he performed. Joe was elated. Hearing Jesus revered by everyone gave him a sense of pride. Myriam must be doing a good job at parenting, and the disciples would protect them from harm by traveling in a group. After a while, Joe decided his concern for them was unfounded.

It was now early spring, and after reaching another village without finding his family, Joe looked north and noticed a mountain in the distance still covered in white. It had been years since he touched snow, and he decided to go and touch it one more time before it melted. After several days, he came to a slope. The temperature was not cold, and the snow was melting fast. Up above the hillside, Joe witnessed something he had never seen before. On the slope were three young soldiers drinking and laughing as one slid down the hill on what looked to be a Roman military shield.

The young man slid perfectly until he lost his balance and tumbled the rest of the way down, kicking up snow and giving his two compatriots something to cheer about.

Joe watched in wonder and decided to approach the soldiers. He was not accustomed to speaking to authority, but he could not resist approaching the lads and getting a better look at what they were attempting to do.

"That looks like fun," Joe said to the soldiers.

"Come, old man, and give it a try," one youth dared. In his sixties but in good shape, Joe resented being called "old," so he took up the challenge. Joe had observed the boy go down the slope leaning forward, causing him to tumble. He also observed a path made from their footprints going up the hill after each attempt was well-trodden. Joe decided to try the path instead of just going down the fresh snow, for it would, theoretically, allow for more stability side-to-side. Joe took the shield in hand and approached the path. He sat down and, leaning back, started his run. Slowly, he gained speed until he was traveling faster than he ever had in his life. The feeling was so exhilarating! The young men cheered and ran after Joe in triumph.

"That was brilliant!" the lads said while gathering around Joe and shaking his hand. Someone produced a waterskin, and a toast was made. The warm liquor felt good after the sled ride. As one of the soldiers took the shield back up the hill, the other two stayed below for a better view.

"What brings you so far north?" Joe asked as the bottle was passed around.

"My father, who commands an outpost in Tiberius, has given us leave. After today, we have to go in search of a man wanted by the Sanhedrin."

Without thinking, Joe asked, "Who's the guy?"

"I had never heard of him before; a man people are calling the Chosen One," one of the soldiers replied in between cheers for his friend, who was now at the top of the hill, ready to come down the path.

"What did this person do?" Joe asked.

"No clue, but we are—come on now, are you going to slide down or stay up there all day?" The soldier talked to Joe and his friend simultaneously and did not explain why. He didn't have to, for Joe felt that pang of fear in his heart as the lad on the top of the hill started his descent. The boys were cheering their friend, who slid down the trail until he lost his balance and tumbled face-first into the snow. Everyone was laughing except Joe, who saw his chance to leave.

"Well, good luck on the search, and thanks for the ride of my life!"

"So long, old man, well played!" the soldiers cheered as Joe mounted the donkey and slowly left the boys to their fun. When Joe felt safe enough away, he put the donkey into a trot. There was a sickening feeling the person the soldiers were looking for was Jesus, and he was desperate to find out.

Chapter 24

Joe headed south and eventually found himself back in Nazareth, where he quickly went to the local prison to check if Jesus had been arrested. As he was about to leave, he was greeted by a familiar voice.

"Hello, Joe."

"Barbee, is that you?"

"Yes, my friend, it has been a long time," replied Barabbas from a small window overlooking the alleyway.

"What are you doing in prison?"

"Long story. Unfortunately, I did something rash. But what brings you here? Not to keep me company, I hope?"

"Myriam's son. I have a feeling he might be in trouble."

"Jesus, you mean?" Barabbas said.

"So, you know his name. I had always suspected," Joe said with bitterness. He still could not get it out of his mind that his friend had corrupted Myriam.

"I can see how you would think the child is mine, but you're wrong, Joe. Do you know why I am in prison?"

"Well, no, I don't understand. You are wealthy and a publican."

"Not anymore. I have been sentenced and will spend the rest of my life here. I thought they would put me to death, but luckily, I had a few of the Sanhedrin who owed me a favor."

"I don't understand, Barbee. You say you are not the father, but I am not that stupid. Jesus is Black; you are Black. Why do you think I gave the child your first name?"

"Joe, listen to me, and you will hopefully understand. When your family fled after the snowball incident, I did what I could to live off the streets, but I needed someplace to stay. There was this man, a man in a very high position, one of the chief priests at the temple, who took a liking to me physically."

"But we were just kids when I left town," Joe interrupted. Then he got the picture of what Barabbas was describing and shuddered in disgust.

"Exactly, that is how he likes them. After a few years, he introduced me to other men in power and government. That is how I got the commission as a tax collector. I traded my soul for a few shekels. Months ago, I saw this man attempt to corrupt another boy no older than I was. I acted rashly and placed a knife in his stomach. Unfortunately, he survived, and now I am here."

"So you and Myriam didn't…"

"Joe, I am so mentally corrupted from being molested as a child that I could never be with a woman. Think back—all the time we spent together—did you ever even see me look at a woman, let alone be with one?"

Joe thought back, and this was true. Barabbas had never been seen with a woman, but there were always men who seemed a little too friendly. Some even gave Joe a queer look that made him uncomfortable. It was all coming back now.

"So, how do you explain Jesus? If you are not the father, then who is?" Joe was still a little cautious because he could not see his friend's facial expressions as they talked.

"I have no idea. There were no Black slaves in the household, not even in the general vicinity. Maybe this was God's way of giving you faith. After all, you never were much of a religious person from what I gathered over time."

"Well, I believe now. Jesus is so kind, just like his mother," Joe replied.

"Yes, and unfortunately, he has her temper as well! It seems Jesus made an example of some moneylenders in the temple. The vendors had special permission to deal there and gave kickbacks to the priests for the prime location," Barabbas replied.

"How do you know this?" Joe asked, stunned by the thought of Jesus causing any act of violence.

"I have my sources. While I am here, some people provide me with information from outside. One of Jesus's disciples, a fellow tax collector, keeps me in the loop. You may know him, a quiet, observant man whose name begins with an M," Barabbas whispered so no one could hear his source of information.

"Yes, I could never figure him out. He was always writing everything down and kept to himself. But why didn't he confide in me?"

"Because he doesn't know that we are childhood friends. Some secrets like that are to your benefit. Trust me on that."

"Well, this explains the soldiers," Joe said, half to himself as he thought about the young boys. They were such good lads, but now they were being sent to arrest Jesus.

"What do you mean, Joe?" Barabbas asked. He could tell that Joe had some information he had not heard of.

"I met some soldiers a few days ago up north who were playing in the snow."

"Same old Joe, you always liked the cold. Now, it seems to have brought more trouble upon you. Who were these soldiers?"

"These are just some innocent lads who said they were told to search for a wanted man and have him arrested. One soldier is just a boy and related to the prefect in Tiberias."

"Yes, I know the Roman you speak of. He is a decent family man who obeys orders. This is good to know. Have you the names of the lads?"

"No, we never exchanged names, but trust me, they are good kids. They allowed me to slide down the hill on their shield."

"Not exactly what I would have done with government property. Did anyone see you doing this?"

"Why, no. Barbee, they didn't do anything wrong. You are not thinking of…?"

"Don't worry, my friend. The information may prove useful someday," Barabbas said while making a mental note to find out who these three individuals were. Sometimes, blackmail can be used for good, and Barabbas was never one for missing an opportunity when it presented itself.

"Barbee, you don't think they will place Jesus in prison?" Joe was fearing the worst.

"Joe, pay attention. From what has been communicated to me, Jesus is being watched by one of the disciples, and all his actions and doings are reported to the high priests at the temple. They are starting to spread the word that Jesus is a criminal and should not be listened to. I have a feeling Jesus will be arrested very soon. The Sanhedrin is ready to try and convict your son now that he has committed a crime."

"Barbee, for years, I was convinced that you and Myriam, well, anyway, after a while, I witnessed things that made me accept what Myriam said regarding God being the father was true. When you see Jesus interacting with others, he is so good, and the boy never thinks about himself; that is why he is in trouble."

"That boy is now a man wanted by the authorities. Find him, Joe, before it's too late, and get him out of Judea. If you need any help, stop by. As you can see, I am not going anywhere."

With that, Joe left his friend and headed directly for home.

Chapter 25

Joe returned home to find Myriam in a panic. Jesus had been arrested and taken away for questioning.

"Oh, Joe, I wish you could have been here. Where were you?"

"I was looking for you both when I got word you might be in trouble. When did they take him?" Joe asked while holding Myriam in his arms. He did not say it, but the embrace felt so good. It had been a long time since he had any physical human interaction. During a crisis, there was no better comfort.

"Joe, I am scared. Lately, it seems there are more people against Jesus than for him. Why the sudden change?"

"I cannot guess, Myriam," Joe said, trying to comfort his wife. But after the conversation with his old friend, he was putting the pieces together. Since Jesus had made a stand at the temple, he was now having the masses turned against him through propaganda and innuendo. Joe had no doubt the Romans had been persuaded to arrest Jesus because of his sudden outburst.

While Myriam and Joe were at home, Jesus was being questioned by the priests.

"What is it that you want of me?" Jesus asked.

"We have several complaints against you for crimes that were committed," the priests stated.

"The only crimes being committed? Are members of this tribunal getting kickbacks from the ones I threw out of the temple" Jesus replied.

"How dare you accuse us of bribery! You are the one on trial here, and your actions cost over thirty shekels in damage."

"Here is the money collected by those who witnessed what happened." Jesus, to the astonishment of the priests, had the exact amount in his hand and gave the money back. "Is there anything else?" As Jesus handed over the money, the priests were at a loss for words. They were not expecting Jesus to be able to repay such a large sum so quickly.

"You can't just come to the temple and take matters into your own hands. What gives you the right to tell us what can't be done?" the priests asked.

"It is God's will what I have done," Jesus said.

"So, you say one cannot conduct business in a place of worship?" the priests asked.

"A place of worship has no need for moneylending, especially when those doing the lending use the temple to prey on those who just came to pray!"

"So, you must also believe that Romans should not collect taxes?" the priests asked.

"God does not need taxes. Caesar taxes everyone to keep the peace, maintain the roads, and provide suitable drinking water. All benefit from these services, and those, including myself, who live under Caesar, pay unto Caesar."

"So, you are a taxpayer and a prophet?" the priests laughed.

"The Roman soldiers protect the neighborhoods and keep the peace. Their pay is drawn from those taxes, but the tax money also goes into the pockets of corrupt politicians."

"So, you are calling the tax collectors crooked as well?"

"You say so, not I."

Finding no fault in his answers, the priests decided to attack Jesus on the subject of race.

"We know you live with a husband and wife who are not Black. Can you explain how you came into their household?" The priests were now trying to get Jesus aroused by attacking his parents. They thought he would admit who his real father was based on the stories they heard. It would trap Jesus into saying something blasphemous.

"My maternal mother raised me without prejudice," Jesus replied.

"But your mother is white. Who is your father? Is not the carpenter also of light complexion? If this is true, then your mother must have had relations with someone else," the priests asked.

"My Father sees all and will judge those when their time comes," Jesus replied.

"From what we have been told, your father is allegedly God above. If this is so, from what you are stating, are we to believe that God himself is Black?"

"You say so," Jesus replied, and he walked out of the temple before guards could be summoned to stop him.

Chapter 26

When Jesus did not return home, word spread that he was now a wanted man. Myriam went into hysteria, but Joe immediately went back to the prison to see if Jesus was incarcerated. After finding that Jesus was not in prison, Joe visited his friend.

"I'm sorry, Joe, but this does not look good. The Romans efficiently find outlaws; if they do not have Jesus in custody already, they will shortly."

"What can I do? Myriam is waiting at home, but Jesus never showed up."

"Well, we will just have to take action before it gets out of hand."

"What do you suggest?"

"Well, the first thing we need to do is get me out of here; otherwise, Jesus will not stand a chance. I know firsthand how a crowd quickly turns into a bloodthirsty mob. That is why Rome has so many games of sport in the arena. By providing a show of gore now and then to quench the mob's lust for blood."

"What do you want to do?" Joe pleaded.

"Come closer; we don't want anyone to hear. Now look, it is Passover, and a custom allows the governor to release a condemned man chosen by the people. So many believe in Jesus that he would surely be chosen as the one to be released, but there is a problem. Once he is arrested, he will be condemned to death by the Sanhedrin. Now, with a few bribes, I will be the one the mob will ask to be released in Jesus's place."

"But how?" Joe asked. He was shocked to hear that Jesus was condemned and that his friend was selfishly placing his own life first.

"Joe, he is condemned for his actions at the temple. They look at him as a threat to all they stand for. I heard from a source that they will make sure Jesus is killed regardless of the governor's decision. People mysteriously die every day while incarcerated. When the time comes, you must walk about the mob, pleading with the crowd not to ask for my release but for Jesus instead."

"Wait, what?" Joe was confused. This was contradictory to all Barbee was saying.

"Joe, you have to trust me on this. Convince the crowd not to release me and to release Jesus instead. When a crowd is told not to do something, they react the opposite way. A mob is easily swayed when aroused and told not to do something; it makes them want to do that deed even more." Joe was still confused, but he listened intently to his friend. He was willing to do anything to save his family.

"Now comes the preparation. Jesus will most likely be sentenced to death by crucifixion. You have seen the method yourself."

Joe thought back to his first order for a cross from the Romans. He was naïve and did not know what it was being made for. Afterward, when he saw the body of the condemned criminal on public display, Joe never made a cross again.

"Joe, pay attention! We need to be one step ahead of the whole process. As a carpenter, you will be chosen to construct the cross for Jesus's crucifixion. I will see to that. Have one ready, but make a hidden support for the body's weight."

"How am I supposed to do that?" Joe asked. He was still bewildered about what Barabbas was trying to plan.

"Joe, I have seen your inventions. Use your imagination, but no one must see the support. Second, you need to get me a heavy concentration of poppies."

After thoroughly reviewing the rest of the plans, Joe left Barbee and quickly made preparations. At home, Joe constructed the cross as asked. After trying it out and being satisfied it would support a body as needed, he dismantled the cross and waited at home, just as he was told. It did not take long for the news to reach them that Jesus had been arrested by the soldiers and incarcerated just as Barbee predicted.

Chapter 27

It was Passover in Judea, and one of the traditions and as a means of good faith to the kingdom was the release of prisoners so they could worship with their families. Pontius Pilate was the governor of Nazareth. He had heard much about Jesus, who was arrested and considered a political prisoner, much like John the Baptist. John, however, was dead, and to appease the mob, Pilate figured Jesus would be chosen by the crowd to be released. Pilate addressed the crowd and stood before them, ready to ask who the Jews wanted to be released from prison. Joe reluctantly started walking among the crowd, pleading like Barbee instructed.

"Don't release Barabbas; release Jesus instead!" Joe pleaded.

The crowd started to mock Joe as he went about in tears, asking everyone with compassion to release Jesus and not Barabbas.

Then Pontius Pilate asked the crowd, "Who do you want me to release?" He figured this would be easy. Jesus had been so famous, and he did not want another uprising in Judea. Once this political prisoner was released, he could go home and forget about any civil unrest during the Passover.

Then Joe quickly started to chant, "Not Barabbas!" louder and louder to the crowd. The more Joe pleased the crowd, the more they laughed at this pathetic man. Eventually, just like his friend had predicted, the crowd started crying, "Release Barabbas!"

"Then it shall be done. I wash my hands of this whole affair," Pontius Pilate said, and he sent for the prisoner to be released. When Barabbas walked out among the crowd, he cheered and yelled in jubilation.

Joe suddenly wondered if this was some kind of trick for the mob to gather around and embrace this man whom they had despised, but now was considered some sort of sadistic hero. When Joe met Barbee's gaze, he was unsure if he had done the right thing. Somehow, he had to place his trust in his friend's plan.

Quickly, Barabbas ran among the crowd, clasping hands and cheering, until he could escape down an alleyway and meet Joe at his home.

"Well, you did it; wonderful job, Joe!" Then he looked around to make sure they were alone. Myriam is at a friend's house as instructed, Joe said.

"How did you know they would release you, Barbee?"

"I didn't, but I took a chance. You must have done a great job in convincing them otherwise. So far, so good. Now for the gruesome part of the plan. Are you up for this?"

"I will do my part if there is any chance of saving Jesus."

"Excellent. You made the cross?"

"Yes, it works as you suggested, but I must assemble it before he is." Here, Joe faltered. He could not even think of nailing Jesus to a cross, let alone anyone else. It was a cruel, barbaric custom, but life was hard under Roman rule and merciless.

As Barabbas examined the cross, he replied, "I knew with your ingenuity it would not be an issue. Perfect. Joe, you have to trust me now. During the crucifixion, do everything I say, and maybe we will be able to save Jesus. Now, when I appear in the mob, ignore me. I will say and do things you do not understand, but again, you must trust me. Do you?"

"I think so," Joe replied. He thought this plan might work as Barbee predicted, but how would it end?

"Good enough answer. Now, how about the poppies I asked for?"

"Yes, here is the packet, but why?"

"Ask no questions. The less you know, the more realistic it will look. Remember, the crowd is easily swayed to hear and see what you want, but you must keep their minds moving; otherwise, they will see through the ruse. Now, I will see you at Golgotha, the place of skulls. That is where they usually take the victims for crucifixion. Farewell, friend."

With a quick look around, Barbee was gone. In the distance, Joe could hear a crowd moving about the city, so he quickly gathered the cross and his tools and dragged the heavy wooden structure toward the noise, stopping and panting to catch his breath. He was getting too old for adventure, but something inside him said that if he did not hurry along, he would never see Jesus again. He kept moving with renewed paternal strength from within and hoped this plan would work.

During this time, Jesus was being led by the mob from prison throughout the town, riding on a donkey. They scattered palms along the pathway and cheered Jesus, praising and mocking the condemned man. Some in the crowd who believed in Jesus and what he stood for were dismayed and kept to themselves, fearing they would share the same fate.

Joe arrived in time to see Barbee personally leading Jesus. When he saw Joe standing there, exhausted, cross in hand, Barbee cried out, "Here, bring that cross to Jesus so he may carry the burden!"

The mob cheered and pulled Jesus off the donkey and made him carry the cross on his way to the crucifixion, spitting and beating Jesus whenever he stumbled.

Joe followed behind in silence but did not interfere. What appalled Joe the most was recognizing some in the mob whom Jesus had assisted financially when they were in need. This was just as Barbee had predicted; they had turned on Jesus and were filled with blood lust. Looking up towards a hill in the distance, Joe noticed two crucifixions had already taken place that morning. The Romans had been busy with their means of justice served.

When Jesus made it to the Mount of Skulls, he was confronted by the two men who had been crucified in the morning but were still alive. One pleaded for Jesus to save them as Joe looked on in tears. How could he go through this task that was brought upon him? He had not felt this low since the child's birth in that filthy manger so many years ago.

While Joe looked on, the crowd removed Jesus's clothes and began casting lots for the condemned man's possessions. Barbee used this time to produce a flask of wine and said it was mixed with gall. To prevent the cup Jesus had made from being taken, he snatched it from the mob's hands and said, "Shall we have the son of God have a drink?"

"Yes!" They all cheered, so Barbee took a jug, poured the wine into the cup, and made Jesus drink all the contents.

The mob cheered again when the cup was held upside down for all to see. Joe watched in disgust and wondered if his friend was acting or enjoying what he was doing.

Barbee now jeered the crowd on, and they asked Jesus to save himself. He kept taunting and challenging the crowd, stalling until it looked like Jesus had passed out. Then Barbee's look changed, and he gave Joe a solemn look as the crowd carried Jesus to the cross. It was time to complete what had to be done. Here, Joe removed the tools from his leather bag and approached the man he had raised like a son.

"Here, old man, let us assist you!" A Roman soldier approached Joe and helped lift Jesus onto the cross. When Joe looked into the young man's eyes, he could not believe it—this was one of the boys he had met from up north. A glance from the boy told Joe it was best not to acknowledge they knew each other. Joe was beginning to feel that maybe, just maybe, Barbee's plan might work.

Now, the gruesome task of nailing Jesus to the cross had to commence. While Joseph was taking his hammer and nails out of his tool bag, he noticed the three young soldiers Joe had met before were there, keeping the crowd at a distance.

Joe looked at the faded, white scar on his hand from the nail he fell on so many years ago. He then placed Jesus' hand on the cross, and with a quick, heavy stroke, to keep the pain to a minimum, Joe sent the sharpened point through the flesh as Jesus cried out in pain.

"Just one more, Jesus. We are hard-working men and can take it," Joe said as he sent the final nail into the other hand.

Barbee cheered when the task was over, keeping the mob distracted. While the soldiers used their shields to prevent the crowd from watching, Joe inserted a peg into the cross to support the body and bound the feet with ropes. The cross was raised and set into a hole; the mob went wild as Barbee kept up the commotion, running around the crowd and getting them to cheer more and more. Then Barbee handed out old fruits and vegetables for them to throw at Jesus, for he knew that without produce, they would search for stones. Just when Joe thought he could take it no more, there was a flash of lightning and a gust of wind that brought dark clouds and rain. Jesus then cried out to God, and then all went silent.

As the rain began to fall, someone poured more of the wine on a sponge, attached it to a reed, and tried to get Jesus to drink, but he did not move. A man approached from the crowd and, taking a spear, prodded the body in the chest, but nothing happened. Jesus was considered dead; the sport was over, and the crowd quickly dispersed to get out of the weather.

Jesus, who devoted his life to helping those in need, was mocked and crucified. God would never forget what they had done.

The crowd felt dread as they went to their homes. What had they done? From that day onward, the people of Judea were doomed for their actions.

As the rain fell on the lifeless body, it washed the blood from his wounds and the filth from the ordeal. Joe looked up to Heaven, tired and numb. The rain blinded his vision as he pondered how the Father could allow this to happen to His son. Barabbas gave Joe time to grieve, put an arm around his childhood friend, and led him away from the gruesome scene.

"This is not over, Joe," Barbee whispered. "Go home and leave the rest to me."

The tone of Barbee's voice gave Joe a strange sense of hope as if Jesus might be resurrected. Mentally exhausted, Joe mechanically packed up his tools and, without looking back, slowly made his way home in the pouring rain to give Myriam the sad news.

Chapter 28

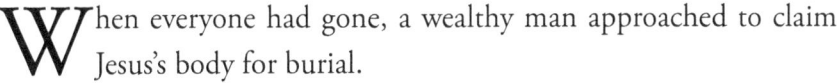

When everyone had gone, a wealthy man approached to claim Jesus's body for burial.

"Barabbas," the man said curtly and with a nod as he approached.

"Ahh, Joseph of Arimathea, right on schedule; thank you for caring about Jesus."

"Pilot says this is the last favor you get; from here on, he can do nothing else to assist… is he?"

"We won't know until we get him down. Have you prepared everything I asked for?"

"Yes, the tomb is prepared as you instructed. I will spread the word about the location in a few days. Luckily, we have this rain that disperses the crowd."

"This rain was no accident, Joseph. I can't explain it, but somehow, it was a miracle this late in the year. I believe that God created the storm to help us. Otherwise, there is no telling what the mob would have done in pleasant weather."

"This is not like you, Barabbas. Never have I heard you speak of God in this way, yourself maybe, but not Him."

"Not now, Joseph, leave my beliefs out of this."

The three young soldiers then lowered the cross, removed the nails from the hands with a tool that was hidden inside Barbee's robe, and wrapped the body in cloth for transport.

"What shall we do with them?" Joseph asked while looking at the two men who were crucified just before Jesus.

"Nothing can be done for them now. One was Need, who stole bread for his family; the other was Want, who stole for personal gain. Only God can help them now," Barabbas said while looking at Need. "The bread he stole wasn't worth a shekel. Anyone in the crowd could have saved that man from this fate, but no one decided to. Then again, they could have saved Jesus but chose to release me instead."

Without another word, Joseph of Arimathea departed with the lifeless body of Jesus as Barabbas thanked the three soldiers for assisting their friend in need.

After the death of their Messiah, the disciples were at a loss. They gathered in a secret meeting hall and discussed what they should do next. The crowd had identified Peter and several other disciples. They were all afraid of being crucified next. There was talk in the streets of more Roman arrests to prevent further civil uprisings.

Jesus walked into the disciples' meeting place three days after the crucifixion. Some were amazed to see him alive again, risen from the dead. Some ran away, afraid of the apparition with the fresh wound on his side and the holes still visible in his hands. Jesus then ate and drank with his disciples for the last time.

"When you break this bread and drink from this cup, you proclaim your commitment to spread the word of God in peace," Jesus said during their last meal together. When the meal was over, the cup Jesus had made by hand was given to them as a reminder of what had transpired.

Before Jesus departed, he warned the disciples not to make the same mistakes as the high priests in the temple and to learn from the corruption that can grow and fester in an organized institution that prioritizes personal gain over assisting others. Then, he bid them farewell and thanked them for their commitment and friendship.

When Jesus departed, word spread that he had risen from the dead. Some were scared of this news, some ignored it, and others would not believe it unless they saw the Son of God in person. The Roman authorities did not believe in the rumor, for the body had been claimed and placed in a tomb. Besides, no one had ever survived a crucifixion before.

The people of Judea went about their daily lives but were never the same after the crucifixion. They were always looking over their shoulders as if something were about to happen.

Chapter 29

"We have a visitor who would like to see you," Joseph of Arimathea said one evening. The sun went down, creating a beautiful sunset through an open window. Birds were chirping outside in the courtyard, and the smell of fresh meat being cooked permeated the air.

"Glad to see you are all safe and sound," Barabbas said.

"Barbee! So glad to see you. Thanks again for all you did. I have to admit that for a while, I was beginning to believe you were enjoying what was being done to Jesus."

"Who says I was not?" he asked while looking at Myriam, who returned the same look of disapproval she had given so many years ago. Then, wiping her hands on an apron, she walked up to Barabbas, kissed him as thanks for what he had done, and departed into the kitchen to finish cooking dinner.

Jesus and Barabbas then met for the first time.

"My family and I are very thankful for what you did, Barabbas. If you repent to God of your past sinful deeds, God will forgive you," Jesus said.

"Why, I never gave it much thought until now," Barabbas said as he sat down and started to clean his nails with a knife.

"Do you condemn what you did in the past?" Jesus then asked.

"For some things, yes; for others, I believe they got what they deserved."

"That is for God to decide, not you, Barabbas. Remember that."

"Well, to me, God seems to have made an awful decision, leaving you there to die on the cross."

"Barbee!" Joe exclaimed.

"Did He? You, a known criminal, risked your life to save mine. I am here now to be known forever as the one who rose from the dead. I tell you this: repent completely in mind and spirit, and God will forgive you for the sins committed," Jesus said.

Barabbas thought about this for a while but was still not convinced God cared about his life. There had been so many hardships growing up. Maybe, on his dying day, he would see things differently and repent.

"I'll think about it," was Barabbas's reply.

"So, what now?" Joe asked his friend.

"Me? I am done with Judea and all its problems. I will take a sea voyage to Pompeii, where they are more receptive to people like me. How about you, Joe? I suggest you all hightail it out of here before word gets out where you are staying."

Joe looked at his wife, who was washing the dishes while Jesus was drying them with a towel. They both stopped what they were doing in the kitchen, waiting for Joe to respond. He had not gotten that look of indecision from either of them for a long time.

"Well, I sure could use a beer."

"Beer?" Jesus asked as if he had never heard the word before.

"Beer, my son. Nothing like it to clear the desert sand from the back of the throat after a long day of travel. How about returning to Egypt and living among the Copts where we were so happy?"

Myriam started to well up; never before had Joe referred to Jesus as his son.

"Sounds like a great idea, Dad," Jesus said, smiling at Myriam—a smile she had seen so many times before, that mischievous smile that her husband made to say everything would be alright.

THE END

www.ingramcontent.com/pod-product-compliance
Lightning Source LLC
Chambersburg PA
CBHW051255170626
46809CB00004B/1666